IN THE EYE OF THE TORNADO

Look for other
DISASTER ZONE books

In the Heart of the Quake

IN THE EYE OF THE TORNADO

DAVID LEVITHAN

AN
APPLE
PAPERBACK

SCHOLASTIC INC.
New York Toronto London Auckland Sydney

ISBN 0-590-12915-5

Copyright © 1998 by David Levithan.
All rights reserved. Published by Scholastic Inc.
APPLE PAPERBACKS and the APPLE PAPERBACKS logo are trademarks and/or registered trademarks of Scholastic Inc.

12 11 10 9 8   12 13 14 15 16/0

Printed in the U.S.A.   40

First Scholastic printing, March 1998

*For Mom, Dad, and Adam
(of course)*

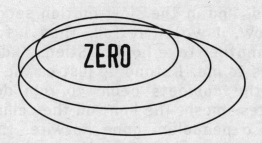

ZERO

My earliest memory:

I am four. My brother Stieg is one and a half. We are living on the outskirts of Portland, Oregon. A small house — two bedrooms, no basement. Our father is away on business. I don't know what his business is, not back then. I know it has something to do with the weather, something to do with storms.

The phones are out. One of the poles has fallen down. Termites have eaten through it. My mother is nervous. She keeps lifting Stieg out of his playpen, then putting him back. She hums a Beatles song and tells me everything is going to be all right. It hadn't occurred to me that things *wouldn't* be all right.

Then the earthquake hits.

It knocks me off my feet. One moment I am standing in the kitchen, making a peanut-butter-and-jelly sandwich. Then the ground buckles. The knife flies from my hand. And in the slow-motion seconds that follow, I watch it fall. Then *I* fall. I see my mother take hold of Stieg. "Adam!" she cries to me. I stand up just as the contents of the cabinets begin to rain down. The plates smash. The light on the ceiling swings like a pendulum gone haywire. My mother grabs at my shirt. I don't even have time to scream.

We stand in the doorway. The kitchen table collapses. The roof will be next. Jars dive off the kitchen counter. Jelly splatters at my feet.

My mother keeps hold of us. She tries to turn my head toward her body. So I'll be protected. So I won't see. But I see everything. I see the faucet burst. I see the refrigerator stumble closer. I see the stairway, the steps unhinging in a tremor. The house is falling apart around us. A piece of the roof lands on the floor above our heads. I can see the dent in the ceiling. I can see there are only moments left.

Then it stops.

Mom waits a moment before letting me go. I turn and see the tears streaming down her face. Even though she battles weather

2

for a living, she can still be scared by earth-
quakes.

I look at Stieg. He's beaming. It is Christ-
mas for him. He's just seen reindeer and
Santa and jingle bells. I expect him to say,
"More! More! More!"

Instead he giggles, "Six-two! Six-two!"

My mother hears this. I see her watching
him, mystified.

"Are you sick, too?" she asks, attempting
an infant translation.

Stieg shakes his head. "Six-two! Six-two!"

The next morning, the newspaper arrives.
The headline reads: "LOCAL QUAKE DEVASTATES
AREA; 6.2 ON THE RICHTER SCALE."

My mother's face turns ash-white when
she sees this.

Six-two. 6.2.

Stieg bobs up and down in his high chair,
pointing at the newspaper.

My mother turns away, turns to me.

"I can't believe it," she whispers, trem-
bling. "Stieg has the Sense."

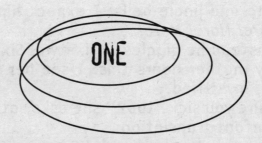

ONE

Our parents are dead now.

Stieg still has the Sense.

My father had the Sense, too. It's the reason he and my mother are dead. It's also the reason hundreds of other people are alive. That's the deal.

My parents drove too close to a tornado. They knew it was coming — that was precisely the reason they were in its path. Someone in the government sent them. Someone who had found out about the Sense. My parents were storm-chasing, trying to get into the eye of the twister in order to plant a military research device. They had done this before, successfully. But this time the tornado turned on them.

This was two years ago, when I was twelve and Stieg was nine. We saw the video on the news, footage taken by another storm-chaser who had stayed farther off. My grand-father tried to stop us from seeing it, but there was no way he could. The video was on all of the TV stations. People saw my parents' truck lift in the air, like Dorothy's house. The twister just sucked them up. They're on screen one moment, gone the next.

My parents are now in Oz. Or the hereafter. Or wherever.

The funeral was one of the biggest the county had ever seen. Because, as I said before, my parents saved many lives. They knew when disasters were going to hit. And they got people out of the way. Simple as that. Members of the Atwood family — ones with the Sense — have been doing it for gen-erations.

Now it's Stieg's turn. Mine, too.

At the funeral, no one said a word. The news people were around, looking for sto-ries. We didn't give them any. Instead, the stories were saved for later, for when Grand-father took Stieg and me back to his house and asked us to stay with him. Grandfather isn't an Atwood himself. But his daughter married one, and she let him in on a few of the family secrets. After the shock of our parents' death had worn off, he told us our mission — something we'd always sus-pected, but hadn't known would come so

soon. He told us we were the last of the Atwood descendants, and he would help us in
any way he could.

Stieg just nodded. He knew.

Perhaps he'd always known.

He is, after all, the one with the Sense.
I am the one with the Chronicles, the Atwood family history, dating back hundreds of
years. This is my job as the oldest. Each
and every book is under my care. New books
await my pen. If Stieg will not write in the
Chronicles, I will. Because sometimes history
is as important as the Sense. Even as science
reaches toward the future, it is built on the
observations of the past.

And with disasters, every piece of information counts.

I learned this for sure when Stieg and I
found ourselves in the eye of a tornado.

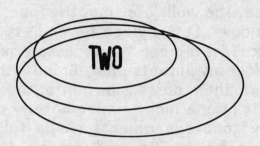

TWO

We live in Grandfather's house. Actually, most of the time we live *under* Grandfather's house. We live in the Maze. Our rooms are deep underground. It's safer that way.

Grandfather's house is a mostly empty mansion, right in the heart of Connecticut. His father was in the oil business at a time when that was the only way to make really big money. The mansion used to be home to ballrooms and billiards and banquets. Now it is home to Grandfather, Stieg, and me. Each of us has a bedroom in the upper house. When Stieg or I have friends over, this is where we sleep. The rest of the time, though, we sleep in our bedrooms underground.

There are eleven rooms in the Maze, and countless secret passages. It is an underground house, a mixture of a mansion and a cavern. Some of the walls have been plastered and papered; video screens simulate sunlight. Other rooms betray the truth of the place. The walls are smooth stone, the walls of a cave. It is a place for endless hide-and-seek. It is a place for necessary secrets.

After my parents died, Grandfather moved all of their possessions into the Maze. He did it in one night, immediately, afraid the books and experiments would fall into the wrong hands. He had reason to worry — the federal agent in charge of my parents' "operation" had begun casing the house during his first condolence call. If my grandfather hadn't acted quickly, our family history would now be in the hands of the person who had sent my parents to their wind-twisted death.

All of the Atwood Family Chronicles now sit safely on the shelves of the Maze's library. Each volume is marked by a date on its cover and a simple word on its spine. *Earthquake* or *Tsunami* or *Volcano*, among others. (Even some that have nothing to do with natural disasters.)

The oldest one dates back to 1843. The last completed volume (prior to Stieg's and my involvement) was finished two months before my parents' accident. They had another book with them in the pickup. Its spine — *Tornado*

— was found fifteen miles from the spot where their truck left the ground. Fifteen miles. The pages were never found. They were scattered. Disintegrated. Dust.

Every now and then, in the two years after my parents' death, I would go into the library and pore over the books, reading random excerpts — stories of devastation and destruction, heroism and escape. Ever since Grandfather had confirmed our mission — ever since I knew for sure that we would be taking our parents' place — I read about the past in order to help brace for the future. Still, I never thought I would need the Chronicles so soon.

The library isn't the only room in the Maze that has to do with the Atwood family calling. Shortly after our parents' accident, I created the Nerve Center. Nobody besides Stieg and Grandfather has ever seen it. It's my place, deep in the heart of the Maze.

You see, having the Sense isn't enough. Premonitions — *feelings* — can't save people on their own. To use them, you need information. And in the case of natural phenomena, you need the best information, as soon as possible. Stieg and I grew up as children of the weather. Or at least I did. Stieg never seemed to care. For as long as I've been able to read, I've been studying floods and storms and glaciers. Especially after it was clear that Stieg had the natural ability for prediction — I knew that information would be my only weapon. Over the years, I acquired a CB radio, a TV with nonstop Weather Channel, and, ultimately, a laptop computer on which I learned to plug into the National Severe Storms Forecast Center, the National Hurricane Center, the United States Weather Service, and other (more renegade) sites.

On the night it all really began, I was sitting in the Nerve Center, studying tidal patterns off the coast of Borneo. At the same time, my modem was receiving storm reports from a scientist in Hawaii whom I'd befriended through my father's E-mail account. It was just another night in the Atwood household. Stieg wasn't paying any attention to me. He was watching MTV on a television set we'd installed in the corner of the Nerve Center, so he wouldn't have to watch continual weather news. In the hallway, I could hear Grandfather wheeling back and forth.

Grandfather's been in a wheelchair for years now — I can't remember him without it. Luckily, the mansion and the Maze were easily made wheelchair-accessible. We don't have any spiral staircases. But we have the most creative ramps ever seen outside of Vegas — there is the Elvis ramp, lined with busts of you-can-guess-who; the neon ramp, which blazes at all hours of the night, causing the Maze to glow; and, my favorite, the Atwood Family Ramp, lined with photos of our parents and all of their predecessors. At the very end of the ramp are pictures of me and Stieg, taking our place in the line.

"So what's the weather supposed to be like two weeks from Wednesday?" Stieg called to me from his corner of the room.

"You know there's no way for me to know that," I answered.

Stieg's eyes didn't veer from the video he was watching.

"I need to know," he said. "That's when summer soccer league starts."

"Chance of showers. Chance of sunshine," I predicted.

"Thanks a lot," Stieg muttered.

"You *know* I can't predict weather two weeks ahead of time," I protested.

"No." Stieg turned to me, away from the MTV. "I don't know that. *You* know that. I don't see what the point is of having all of this satellite information if you can't tell what the weather's going to be like."

"Just wait and find out," I said. But that was the problem — Stieg doesn't like to wait and find out. He wants immediate answers. He loves the *now* of things.

This gets Stieg into trouble. Mrs. Hailey, his sixth grade teacher, requested (twice) that

11

he be transferred from her class. She gave him an F for his class project, "The Secret Life of Charlie Brown." Granted, the assignment had been to profile a Significant National Figure. But Stieg's argument (that presidents come and go, while Charlie Brown always remains the same) didn't really fly with most of the Middle School Powers That Be. Luckily, Stieg's guidance counselor has a sense of humor. Otherwise, Stieg might have been booted back to fifth grade. If not third. Mrs. Hailey has labeled Stieg a "slow learner." But I think the truth of the matter is that he's too fast for everyone else — nothing can hold his attention for that long. I always find myself trying to keep him in line.

"Have you done your homework yet?" I asked him (not for the first time) as I received my communications from Honolulu.

"Homework's for losers," Stieg answered with a smile. "No offense."

I turned back to the satellite feed of Borneo. I had just noticed a slight coastal disturbance when Grandfather called us in to dinner.

Stieg turned off his television set. I left the computers running.

On our way out of the room, Stieg said to me, "Seventy-three, with partial cloud covering and fifty-four percent humidity."

"What?" I asked.

"Two weeks from this Wednesday. The weather. Just a guess."

Stieg seemed as surprised by this prediction as I was.

"How do you know that?" I asked, even though I knew the answer.

"It just came to me," he explained. "Just one of those flashes."

That's what he called the Sense's premonitions: "those flashes." Up to that point, they had hit him infrequently. When they did, it was rarely about anything important.

"Jealous?" Stieg said with a smirk.

I wanted to hit him. I *was* jealous of the flashes. But instead of retaliating, I pushed Stieg into the Maze's kitchen.

Grandfather was waiting for us at the head of the table. The three of us have a deal: He cooks, we serve and clean. In the kitchen, a pan of lasagna and two loaves of garlic bread sat on the low-lying counter.

"Got another phone call today," Grandfather announced as the food was passed around. "The Hansen family. From Providence. Wanted to see how you were doing."

When Mom and Dad died, they left us many things. Mom left us a large inheritance, which means that Stieg and I will be "financially independent" for the rest of our lives. (Each of us has an ATM card that we can use at any time, at our own discretion.) Dad left us our Atwood family history, as well as our Atwood family traits. Mom and Dad both gave us a sense of responsibility to help people, especially in the face of disaster. To make this easier, we were also willed a large number of people whom Mom and Dad had met, befriended — and sometimes saved. These were the people who came to the funeral. These are the people who have called to check up on us in the years since. They offer us any help they can give. We don't often take it. But it's nice to know that it's there. We call these people the Network.

"Did you tell the Hansens that we're clone addicts, and that I now have seven Adam clones to organize my record collection?" Stieg asked, dipping some of his garlic bread into tomato sauce.

"No," Grandfather replied, not missing a beat. "I told them I'd abandoned you to the woods, to be raised by wild turkeys."

Stieg gobbled in response. With his mouth full. Not a pretty sight.

Then his face turned as pale and shadowed as the full moon. He gasped for air. I was sure he was choking.

"Stieg — what is it?" Grandfather yelled. I jumped up, ready to perform the Heimlich maneuver, but Stieg waved me away.

"What? What?" Grandfather and I both

14

asked. Stieg's mouth opened, but he was struck mute. He closed his eyes. Then he opened them and blinked rapidly. I leaned over to touch his shoulder, but he pulled away. I looked at Grandfather, who seemed as mystified as I was.

Stieg's hands flew to his face and covered his eyes. He began to rock back and forth. Then, as if he'd just been stung, he jumped out of the chair. It crashed to the floor. Stieg didn't seem to notice — he was bolting out of the room, before Grandfather and I could even turn our heads to follow. I heard his footsteps echo through the hall of the Maze. I heard his door slam. I heard him fall to the floor.

Before either of us could say a word, I left Grandfather in the dining room. The hallway was dark, but I could see the slight crack under Stieg's door. It cast a shadow of light, which spread toward me and drew me in.

When I touched Stieg's doorknob, a shock of electricity jumped to my finger.

Opening the door, I found Stieg sitting on the floor, furiously attacking a sketch pad with a pen. His blond hair nearly covered his eyes. He wrote anyway.

I looked over his shoulder. The lines — some were arrows, some were lines — didn't make sense. "Stieg," I said. Then a little louder, "STIEG." But he didn't turn. He slouched further over the pad, continuing with his mad geometry. There was something that looked like a woman in the corner of the paper. But I couldn't be sure.

Stieg would not relent. He turned the page sideways and upside down, to find free space. I sat down beside him. When his pen began to break under his hand (sharded plastic, bleeding ink), I gave him a new one. Then, as abruptly as he'd begun, Stieg stopped. He collapsed. He lay back on the floor and took deep breaths.

"Are you okay?" I asked repeatedly. His eyes were closed. I wondered if he even knew I was there.

Then his eyes opened. He stared at me, and I knew I was registering. In the folds of a breath, he whispered, "Tornado."

Tornado.

All at once, I knew what was happening.

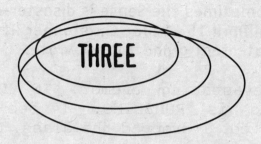

THREE

The Sense.

Sometimes it arrives violently. Other times, you have to strain to feel it.

Since I don't have the Sense myself, I only know this secondhand. Not so much from Stieg as from the Chronicles. The words of the Atwood family past.

"Imagine you are sitting in a room," my father wrote in the Chronicles when he was twenty-two. "You hear the voice of someone else in the room. He could be shouting, or whispering. You look around and find that there's no one there. You realize that the person, the voice, is *inside your head*. And once you realize this, he will not stop talking. He is all you can hear. The rest of your senses

shut down. Sometimes you can understand him. Sometimes you can't. No
matter what, you can't make him go
away."

Sometimes the Sense is disaster-specific.

On April 15, 1906, Christopher Atwood (my
great-great grandfather) wrote:

Devastating tremor. IN MY MIND.
Mind is RUMBLING. I see things
tilted. I dropped the glass. My hands
are shaking.

This was three nights before the San Francisco earthquake.

Seven years earlier, he wrote:

DROWNING. Vision BLURRED. Legs won't
work, pulled backward even as I walk
forward. CANNOT BREATHE. Sounds are
distant. Marybeth is calling me. She
is five feet away. It seems like
miles. Unsteady. Full of water.

This was five days before the Johnstown
flood — the most damaging flood in U.S. history at that time.

(Both times, my great-great-grandfather
was able to make it to the disaster sites on
time. No small feat at the turn of the last
century.)

We did not know how the Sense would affect Stieg — not until Grandfather and I watched him turn pale in the light of the Maze. While he could predict the weather without strain, he had never before had an *attack* of the Sense. Not while our parents had been alive. Nor immediately afterward, when I had feared for a short time that Stieg and his "gift" had shut down entirely. (For a year, he wouldn't speak of the weather, or talk about our parents, or laugh.)

Now the Sense was upon him.

As he gasped the word *tornado*, I looked to the doorway and found Grandfather in his chair. He, too, immediately understood.

A minute passed, and Stieg began to breathe more normally. Grandfather called his name lightly. Stieg turned to look. Their eyes — equal blue — met.

"Do you know where it will happen?" Grandfather asked gravely.

Stieg shook his head *no*.

"Do you have an *idea* of where it will happen?"

Stieg nodded.

"Do you know when it will happen?"

Stieg nodded again. Then, regaining his voice, he whispered, "Two days."

"What?" Grandfather asked.

"Two days," Stieg answered again, his voice more sure of itself.

"Two days," Grandfather repeated, scratching his chin. "We have to get started right away. We have a lot of work to do. *Now.*"

That was it.

There could be no delay.

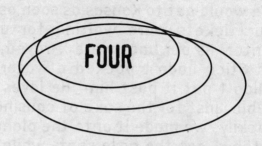

FOUR

Kansas.

We were on our way to Kansas.

Hours after Stieg had experienced the Sense, we were at the airport, on the first flight of the morning. Grandfather had urged us to sleep, but it had been a restless night of preparation. My backpack held some clothes, my laptop, my modem, and a half-dozen Chronicles marked *Tornado*. Stieg had his Walkman on. He was acting as if this were just another family trip.

Except it wasn't a family trip. Grandfather wasn't coming. He no longer drove. He rarely left the house. Anyway, he trusted us. And, in a way, he didn't have a choice. He would call our school and make our excuses. He would cover for us. He had to. It was possible that lives were held in the balance.

"I'd only slow you down," he had said before we both hugged him good-bye.

We would call. We would send him messages over the computer.

We would get to Kansas as soon as possible.

Our tickets were waiting for us at the counter. As our bags were X-rayed, I prayed that Stieg hadn't packed a water pistol. I wouldn't put it past him. He loves to cause trouble, just for the sake of causing trouble.

Luckily, we made it onto the plane without a hitch. I got the aisle seat, while Stieg sat by the window. I used to get the window seat. When I was little, I would identify the clouds as we flew through — *cirrus, cumulonimbus, stratus* — all magical words. I would say these words out loud. The adults around me found this endearing . . . for about two minutes. Then they began to look as if they wanted to smother me. I was soon moved to the aisle seat, and had been placed there ever since.

Stieg didn't care one way or another. He never looked out the window. He closed the shade and watched the movie, even when it wasn't a movie at all — just an in-flight news broadcast, or a telemagazine about the Wonders of Glorious Portugal. (If it's on a screen, Stieg can digest it. I prefer to flip pages.)

After we took off, I made Stieg put away

his Walkman. We had to talk, big-time. I had to tell him about tornadoes.

Even under the circumstances, Stieg was hardly a ready and willing student.

"What do you know about twisters?" I asked, my tray in the fold-down position, a sketch pad atop it.

"Not much," Stieg sighed. "I must have been absent for that class."

"Do you know how a twister is formed?"

"Well, a mommy twister and a daddy twister come together and . . ."

I was going to have to start with the basics.

I drew a diagram of cold air hovering over warm air.

"Basically," I explained, "this is how it begins. In a storm front, where the cold air meets the warm air. Now, warm air rises and cold air sinks. Right?"

Stieg nodded.

"Well, in twister conditions, the warm air exists *below* the cold air. The warm air is trying to rise. The cold air won't let it. The cold air, in turn, is trying to sink. But the warm air won't let it, either. So they fight.

23

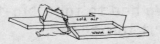

"The storm starts, in a big way. The warm and the cold winds swirl against each other, pushing and shoving. Finally, the warm, moist air gets strong enough to punch a hole in the cold air. It rises and is frozen by high-speed winds, forming clouds and rainstorms — sometimes hail. The clouds can be thunderheads twice the height of Mount Everest. A mesocyclone — a spinning column of air, a funnel cloud a few miles wide — can form. Now, two things can happen. Either the funnel cloud goes away. Or it will drop down to the ground, spinning. The first thing you see is the bottom of the mesocyclone, the wall cloud — a darker, spinning cloud, coming from the bottom of the thunderhead. This is when you know you're in trouble. Seconds count. Because the twister has formed.

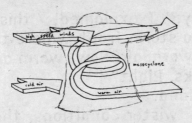

"When the twister touches down, it does so from a height of fifteen thousand to twenty thousand feet. That's over three thousand times as tall as you. Its winds can blow up to three hundred miles per hour. People think that a twister is one big funnel, and it's this single funnel that does all the damage. But that's not necessarily the case. Because within each tornado, there are many different suction vortices — little twisters within the tornado. These are the things that cause the most damage. They are incredibly unpredictable — there is no way to anticipate where they will fall. They strike without any respect to logic or reason. The suction vortices can pull the roof off a house without moving any of its furniture.

"The rain from the tornado causes another blast of cold air, which either ends the mesocyclone or generates its own wind shear, causing a new tornado. Eventually, it's over. Damage is inevitable. This," I concluded, "is what we are running toward."

I opened up the Chronicles and turned to a page I had marked. My fingertips traced the loops and lines of my great-grandfather Jacob's handwriting:

Murphysboro, Illinois. March 18, 1925. Unbelievable destruction. I have never seen a whole town destroyed. But it is so. Nothing left. Over 200 dead. Violently. The ground is scattered with limbs and branches. Human limbs — it is too

distressing to say more. Caught un-
prepared. Nothing to do. Men screaming for wives. Buildings toppled.
Some have disappeared — torn apart,
unrecognizable. Chairs sit in trees,
bodies below them. I saved five families — warned them, made them go
into cellars and bolt shutters. But
is that enough? Can that ever be
enough? An Ede got here first,
didn't help much. Death everywhere.

I let Stieg read these words silently. I
made him read them twice. Then I turned to
another marked page — our father's handwriting, from when he was seventeen, only
three years older than me. Stieg grew pale
and turned away.

"You have to," I whispered.

It was important that he see these words.
It was important that he feel the link to our
father, that he know enough to be afraid of
tornadoes and not of our father's pen.

"Look," I said, pushing the Chronicles into
his lap.

He turned back to me, but would not look
at the book.

"I wouldn't ask you to if I didn't think it
was necessary," I assured him. "If you don't
read this now, we might as well turn right
back around. It's the most important lesson

an Atwood can learn. Our father learned it when he was young. We're going to learn it when we're younger. It's almost as if he wrote it down for us."

Stieg reluctantly lifted the book and began to read:

I have seen people fly. I have seen them lifted off the ground. One woman was no more than ten feet away from me. Her hair had been braided tightly. But as the tornado lifted her, the braids came undone. She was carried into the sky, shrieking. Her shriek became the tornado's. She was followed into the wind by a stairway, then a porch. She landed one hundred feet away. Still breathing. Barely breathing. A lamp had hit her as she fell.

It is April 12, 1965. Yesterday, thirty-six tornadoes hit six states. I barely made it to Wisconsin. I arrived just as the funnel dropped. I ran from my car and watched as it was thrown into the window of a hotel. A few seconds separated my life from death. A few feet. Maybe inches.

And I was too late to help. I was only in time to put myself in danger. Taking shelter and watching as trees were uprooted and a shoe flew in

the air (whose?), I realized: We are
not here to stop disasters. Then the
lady with the braids left the ground.
Some of her hair landed at my feet.

There is no way to stop a tornado.
We can arrive weeks ahead of time,
and things will still be destroyed.
The best we can do — the *only thing
we can do* — is to save lives and
lessen the damage. If we try to stop
the thing from happening, we will
either kill ourselves in the process
or go crazy from thinking about what
we might have done differently.

It is the number one rule of the
Sense. I write it now to remind myself. I also write it for future
generations. <u>We cannot destroy Na-
ture. We can only try to prevent Na-
ture from destroying us.</u> That's all.
And that's something.

"Okay. Whatever," Stieg said as he handed
the book back to me. I tried to see if our father's words had sunk in. But I couldn't read
Stieg as easily as I could read the Chronicles.
He put his Walkman back on. He didn't seem
to be afraid — and I wanted him to be afraid.
We were going to be facing some fearful el-
ements. A respect for their power would be
essential.

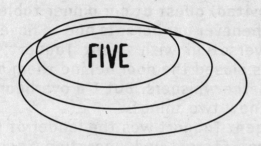

FIVE

We were expecting the Wachsteters to meet us at the airport. Our parents had saved them from a hurricane when they had lived on the Georgia coast. The Wachsteters had soon after moved to Kansas, to be away from hurricanes forever. (Of course, the move had placed them squarely in the tornado and dust bowl belts — but such are the perils of living in America: You move from one disaster area to another, wherever you go.)

Grandfather had called the Wachsteters as soon as he learned our destination. They were part of the Network, and were eager to help in any way possible.

Our plane landed early. The Wachsteters hadn't made it to the gate area yet.

Instead, someone else was waiting for us. The worst possible alternative.

I saw him first. Then Stieg stopped short and I knew that he, too, had seen Agent Taggart. We could recognize him easily enough. He had been a frequent (mostly uninvited) guest at our dinner table.

Whenever our parents had to have a private conversation with Agent Taggart, they always closed the door behind them and spoke in fierce whispers. But I'd overheard enough to know two things:

Agent Taggart was the leader of Operation Secret Storm. And Operation Secret Storm was the reason my parents were dead.

Really, that's all I needed to know.

Stieg knew this, too. Without a word, we both started to run. But I only made it a few yards before I felt a hand grab my shoulder tightly. I looked up and saw a man in a suit, grinning. Stieg put up more of a fight — kicking and screaming, "GET OFF OF ME!" One of the flight attendants from our plane headed toward us, looking concerned. But Agent Taggart flashed his badge and made excuses. Stieg was relentless. He bit the hand of the man who held him. Agent Taggart gave orders for us to be taken to the Safe Room.

We were in trouble. Big-time.

The Safe Room was an abandoned airport lounge. Stieg and I were told to sit on an orange vinyl couch — vintage waiting-room furniture — until Agent Taggart could "attend to" us. The two agents who had grabbed us guarded the door. There weren't any windows.

Stieg had calmed down, but I could tell he was just waiting for his moment.

The guards assured us that Agent Taggart only wanted to talk to us. As if that had been his cue, Taggart strode into the room. He was smiling. Which was a bad sign. Stieg had just bitten one of his men and had caused a scene. There was no reason for Agent Taggart to smile.

Except, I guess, for the fact that he'd captured us.

"Why?" I asked. I hadn't meant to say it out loud. But there it was. Why?

"A good question," Taggart said as he pulled over a green vinyl chair to sit across from us. It was a reply, not an answer.

Stieg avoided Taggart's eyes, choosing instead to look at the bleached-out travel posters behind the federal agent's head. As if cheap airfare to Miami held more interest than the predicament we were in.

Taggart glared fiercely, trying to unnerve us. I studied him closely — the man who had trapped my parents, and who had led them to their death. His eyes were gray. His hair was dyed black. (You weren't supposed to notice, but I could tell.) There weren't any rings on his fingers. I remembered my mother saying that Taggart's job was all the family he needed.

Sensing Stieg's brick-wall attitude, Taggart directed his words toward me. I had no choice but to listen.

"I can't blame you for wondering why I have you here," he began. "Believe me, my intention had been to ask you to talk for a little while. That's all. That scene at the gate could have been avoided. I don't know what you know about me or about what I do." He flashed his badge. "I am Agent James Taggart of the U.S. Government. You can call me Jim, if you wish."

"No thank you," Stieg muttered.

Agent Taggart continued unfazed. "As your parents may or may not have told you, I work on Operation Secret Storm, a highly classified project to which your parents devoted countless time and energy."

And their lives, I added mentally.

"Operation Secret Storm is vital to our national security. I don't need to tell you that he who controls the weather, controls the world." Taggart paused for dramatic effect, then resumed. "Now, we have reason to believe that the two of you have your parents' gift for meteorological . . . speculation. It is thus of natural interest to us when you de-

32

cide to make hasty travel arrangements, as you have done today."

"We're visiting a sick relative," I explained.

Agent Taggart flashed a chilly grin.

"You don't have any relatives in Kansas," he said. "Believe me — we would know if you did."

"And how did you know we were coming?" I had to ask.

"Let's just say that we knew, and leave it at that. The reason we are here is to ask for your help. We all want the same thing: to save lives and to prevent massive damage. We're on your side. Teammates. And right now we need you on the field."

I recalled various entries in the Chronicles, entries my father had written in the years before his death. "Taggart is very persistent. Too persistent." "Taggart isn't from the Weather Bureau, as we were led to believe. I don't trust him." "It seems easier to go with Taggart than to try to stop him. There's no avoiding him. He could make trouble. And he's not asking too much. Not yet, at least." "Must remember: *Beware of Taggart.* All is not as it seems."

Now we were caught in Taggart's web. He paused again, to stare searchingly into our eyes. I looked away, but Stieg matched him glance for glance. Then Stieg began to shake his head: *No way.*

"We *know* that you can predict the weather," Taggart stated, his eyes still locked on Stieg's. "Some people in our bureau even believe you can *control* the weather. You are a vital part of our operation. The sooner we get down to work, the better."

Stieg and I were silent. It wasn't as if we were being given a choice, although Taggart wanted us to think we were.

"Rothman," he said to the agent who had grabbed my arm, "go bring the car around." Agent Rothman took out his keys and raced out of the room.

"Now, kids." Taggart turned his steely gaze to us once more. "Where is our destination? The sooner we know, the better."

There was a moment's pause before I answered.

"Springfield," I said flatly, even though I had no idea where we were going. "We're going to Springfield, Kansas."

Taggart nodded. If Stieg felt any surprise at my bluff, he didn't show it.

"Thank you," Taggart said, flipping open a pad and writing a few words down. "Now, I know this is happening very suddenly. I'm sure you appreciate the urgency of the situation. I have to go make some phone calls. When I return, we'll discuss our plans for you. We have a certain experiment in mind. One very similar to the ones your parents were a part of. Only a little more . . . intense. As soon as this situation is over, I assure you that we'll have you back with your grandfather in no time. Everything will go back to normal. We'll never bother you again."

Taggart stood to leave.

"Agent Cha — keep an eye on them. I'll be back shortly."

As the door closed behind Taggart, I thought about what he had said. Especially the last part, about returning to Grandfather's. As if everything could go back to normal. I *knew* that it wouldn't. And I knew that Taggart understood this, as well.

He was lying.

I had no doubt he would lie again.

I looked at Stieg to see his reaction. His jaw was clenched. His eyes were icy. He had no intention of giving in. Of the two of us, he had more to lose. As soon as they figured out he was the one with the Sense, he would fall under the microscope. I would be the accessory. He would be the experiment. And if some people thought that he could actually *control* the weather, as Taggart had said . . . well then, Stieg could kiss a normal life good-bye. He'd spend his days beneath laboratory light. My father had been safe because he had been an adult when Taggart came calling — people would have noticed his disappearance. But we were just children. Orphans. Open targets.

"What are we going to do?" I asked quietly. I could see Agent Cha straining to hear Stieg's answer.

"Adam, I don't feel too good," Stieg replied. Loud enough for Agent Cha to comprehend.

"What's wrong?" I asked.

Stieg started to wheeze.

"Can't . . . breathe . . . too . . . good," Stieg gasped. I was alarmed.

Then I saw Stieg's wink.

A-ha.

"Where's your inhaler?" I yelled frantically. I grabbed for our bags. Agent Cha jumped at this sudden movement. He asked if something was wrong.

"My brother — he's having an attack," I explained.

"Left . . . inhaler . . . on plane," Stieg shuddered.

"What?" Agent Cha asked.

"He left it on the plane!" I exclaimed. "I have to go get it. *He could die* if he doesn't have his inhaler."

I started to run for the door, but Agent Cha yelled at me to stop.

"Don't move," he commanded. Stieg fell to the floor and began to writhe. I prayed he wouldn't hurt himself while pretending to be hurt. "I'll go get the inhaler. I'm locking the door. Stay here."

With that, he was gone. I heard the door bolt behind him. There was no way to unlock it from inside. *That* was why it was called a Safe Room. It was a dressed-up prison cell.

Stieg continued to wheeze and groan for a minute or so, just in case Agent Cha had stopped to listen. We were running on borrowed time. Stieg and I looked around for a way to escape — and found an air vent at our feet. Stieg reached into his bag for his Swiss Army knife and quickly unscrewed the screen from the duct. The passageway was barely large enough to fit Stieg — I wasn't sure I'd make it. But I really didn't have a choice. Our bags had to be dragged behind us. There was no question about which direction we would take. There was only forward.

It was impossible to escape quietly — the metal walls reverberated with our every move. So we opted for speed over silence. We only had a minute or two before one of the agents discovered our disappearance. The duct into which we had escaped met up with a larger passageway. We pushed our way forward as cobwebs clung to our faces and dirt covered our clothes. We had to get as far away as possible, as soon as possible.

We peered down each vent we came to,

looking for a way out. Then we saw sunlight. Hurriedly, Stieg and I crawled toward its source. We were at the baggage docks. A uniformed security guard walked right in front of us. Stieg and I pulled back before we could be seen.

"Here?" Stieg whispered. I nodded. There wasn't time to try anywhere else.

I pressed my face to the screen. When I saw that nobody was coming, I motioned to Stieg. With four quick twists of the knife, he had the screen detached. Stieg and I sprang out. We were right by the conveyor belt that carried luggage into the baggage claim. Far off, I could see a cargo shuttle approaching. We were locked in its path.

We were stuck. I was paralyzed. Stieg pulled me by the sleeve.

"I've always wanted to do this," he muttered. He jumped onto the baggage belt. I followed.

It wasn't moving, but it led in the right direction. From behind us, I could hear an airport employee cry, *"Hey, you!"* Stieg and I ran up the belt, parting the carwash-style curtain in order to enter the airport. Luckily, the passengers had yet to arrive for their luggage. But we sure got some strange looks from the porters and limo drivers. "Security?" one of them called. It was more of a question than a cry for help. Stieg and I kept running.

The airport doors opened before we could touch them. I headed left — but then I saw Taggart, standing no more than a hundred feet away. I could tell he already knew of our escape. I turned right and struck gold: a taxi stand. I lunged into the nearest cab, pulling Stieg behind me. Agent Taggart had spotted us. I could hear him yelling. As I looked through the cab's windshield, I could see him beginning to run in our direction.

"GO! NOW!" I screamed. The taxi driver switched on his blinker and began to move into the traffic lane. Taggart was almost at our side.

Stieg reached into his pocket and threw a fifty-dollar bill at the driver.

"NOW!" he repeated. The taxi swerved away from the curb. Taggart grabbed at the door handle. But he was too late. The car pulled away from him. I could see Stieg staring him down. *We win,* Stieg's glare said. But I could tell from the look on Taggart's face that he wasn't going to go away.

Not now. Not ever.

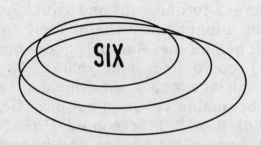

SIX

We had to get out of the cab as soon as possible. Taggart was sure to be reporting the license plate and cab number to the authorities. It was only a matter of minutes before we'd be traced.

A voice on the cabbie's CB radio asked where he was. Taggart had no doubt taken down the name of the cab company as well. The cabbie, for whatever reason, didn't answer his dispatcher. Perhaps he saw our condition — breathless, ragged, dirty — and decided not to turn us in. Maybe he had seen the look on Taggart's face and figured out that we were the good guys. (The fifty dollars couldn't have hurt, either.) Whatever the case, we knew then that we could trust the cabbie. And that, in turn, saved us.

I asked the cabbie to drop us off at the

nearest bus station. Upon arriving there, we wished him well and tipped him an extra fifty. Inside the terminal, we bought tickets on the earliest possible bus, leaving in five minutes. We ran onboard and slunk low in our seats.

"I hope it doesn't stop in Springfield," Stieg said, remembering the town I'd given Taggart as our destination.

"I don't even know if there *is* a Springfield, Kansas," I confessed. "I just know that Springfield is the most common town name in America. It seemed like a good bet."

I expected Taggart and his men to come crashing into the terminal at any moment — to surround our bus with guns drawn, ready to whisk us away to some secret underground laboratory. It wasn't until we were out of the Wichita city limits that I began to breathe normally.

If Stieg was worried by our situation, he didn't let it show. "Onward toward tornadoes," he proclaimed calmly, reaching into his bag and pulling out the sheet he had drawn on while he'd been caught up in the Sense.

"Do you know now where we're supposed to go?" I asked. Up until then, all he'd been able to say was *Kansas*.

"No," Stieg shook his head, "but I have a

feeling the answer's on this piece of paper.
This is my map. It has to be."

I looked down at the paper. It didn't look
like a map to me. In fact, it didn't look like
anything, other than scribbling.

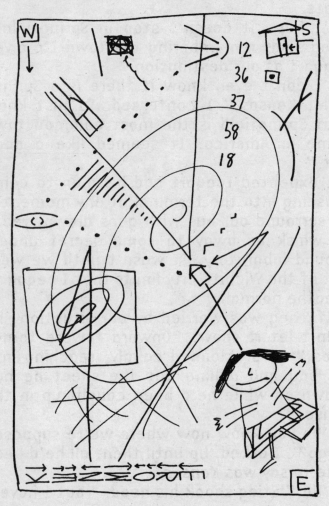

I pointed to the series of arrows in the lower left-hand corner of the paper. "Do you think these lead the way?" I asked.

"Sure, if we only knew where the starting point was."

"Maybe the arrows have something to do with the lines above them."

Stieg shrugged. "Whatever. Can I sleep now?"

I didn't even bother to answer. Stieg would need his rest, anyway. As he dozed, I scrutinized the map. In the seat behind me, a middle-aged man chewed loudly on a wad of gum. Across from Stieg, an elderly lady knitted. Whenever the bus hit a bump, she paused for a moment and rested her needles in her lap. Then, when the turbulence had passed, she resumed. All very orderly.

I looked at the arrows again. I hoped we were traveling in the right direction. Out the window, all I could see were endless waves of cornstalks. An occasional barn. Cows. Every mile seemed the same.

I took out my computer and booted it up. I wished there was some way I could connect my modem, just to tell Grandfather we were okay. (By now, the Wachsteters would have arrived at the airport to find us missing. I wondered what, if anything, Agent Taggart was saying to them.) I also wondered what my friends were thinking as they saw my empty desk at school. Would I rather have been there? Not really. Stieg was more likely to miss his friends than I was.

My laptop beeped and purred. I turned away from the screen and looked once more out the window. I saw the faint shadow of my face and tried to wipe some of the dirt off my forehead. I could see Stieg's reflection next to mine. I could see Stieg sleeping, and wondered what he dreamed.

The Sense had ruined my father's sleep. From my bed, I could hear him wander around the house in the middle of each night, restless and insomniac. From an early age, I wondered when it would start to happen to me — the nightmares, the premonitions. I had only a vague idea of what the Sense was. I wanted to be ready for it. I never thought that it would pass me over completely.

Looking at Stieg asleep on the bus, I could see traces of our mother. The curl of her hair. The lines of her smile. It wasn't fair. Stieg looked like my mother. I looked like my father, like an Atwood. I was the oldest. I was the more willing. And yet, I was without the Sense. Many nights, I had tried to conjure it. I sat absolutely still in a deathly quiet room. I strained to hear the voices. I urged my senses to extend, to somehow *know*. But all I could feel was emptiness. I could learn everything there was to know about disasters, about natural phenomena — and part of me would still (always) be hollow. Stieg had it. I didn't. It was as simple and as complicated as that.

I stared at the blank computer screen, wondering what it was that I wanted to do. I was about to start a letter to Grandfather when suddenly my seat began to rock back and forth. At first, I thought the man behind me was kicking forward. Then I turned to Stieg and found that he was sitting up straight, banging against his armrest.

His eyes were still closed.

"Stieg?" I asked, moving to touch his hand. He pulled away. He began to grasp at his hair. The lady with the knitting needles shot me an alarmed glance. I moved my arm around Stieg's shoulders and began to talk to him quietly. Soothingly.

His eyes shot open.

"What is it?" I asked.

"Stop the bus," he said hoarsely. *"We have to stop the bus."*

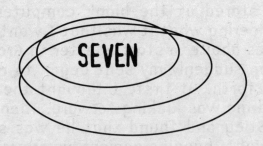

SEVEN

There were only a dozen people on the bus, most of them elderly. I'm sure all of them heard Stieg's shout.

"Stop the bus *now*!" he cried. I packed up my laptop, ready to follow his next move.

"What is it?" I asked.

"Tornado. We're in its path."

"What's going on back there?" the bus driver yelled. I could see him glaring at us in his rearview mirror.

Stieg was out of his seat in a flash. I paused for a moment and looked out the window. The sky was growing darker. The cornstalks bent further under the wind.

I couldn't see a mesocyclone yet. But these were the conditions. An unsteady storm front. No rain yet. A shot of lightning in the distance.

I ran to the front of the bus. It had started to rain. Stieg was trying to convince the bus driver to turn around.

"Yeah, right, kid," the driver said. The tattoo on his arm read BUTCH. "Look, if you gotta throw up, go in the bathroom in the back. I can't pull over. And I *can't* turn around."

"There's a storm coming. Tornadoes," Stieg explained.

"Nothing 'bout that on the radio," the driver muttered. "How do you know?"

"I just know," Stieg said.

The driver merely grunted in response.

"Nothing but a bad storm," he said, turning on his windshield wipers.

"Sit down already!" the man who'd been seated behind us hollered. I looked at the other passengers. They were all paying attention, but none of them seemed inclined to help. Short of hijacking the bus, there was no way we could make it turn around.

Stieg and I stayed by the driver. I tried to gauge the storm's direction. Most tornado systems appear in the southwest quadrant of a storm.

The clouds were growing more sinister. Daylight had become twilight in a matter of minutes. The road stretched out before us. We were the tallest thing around — a prime target for a twister. Beside the road, there was a deep ravine. And beyond that, miles of empty farmland.

"You've got to stop," Stieg said calmly. But the driver wasn't going to listen to us.

"Go back to your seats," he ordered. But there wasn't enough time.

The clouds began to swirl.

"Holy — " The driver slowed the bus.

I looked to the sky, mesmerized.

From the height of the clouds, baseballs began to fall. Only they weren't baseballs. They were pure ice. Hailstones. Rock-hard, they began to pelt the bus. Lightning lit the sky.

"Everybody down!" Stieg yelled. There was no time to evacuate. The hail, traveling at a speed of sixty miles an hour or more, was denting the roof of the bus. The man who'd been sitting behind us screamed. Other passengers fell into the emergency crash position, hands over head, head over knees.

The driver put the bus in reverse and began to speed backward.

"No," Stieg cried. "You can't outrun it. It's too close."

His eyes darted across the landscape.

"The ditch! You have to pull over into the ditch!" Stieg ordered.

"It won't fit!" the driver protested.

"MAKE IT FIT!" Stieg yelled.

I braced myself against the dashboard. A bulge was forming on the bottom of the dark, high, swirling cloud. Any moment, the funnel would drop.

But where?

Tires screeched against pavement.

"Hold on!" the driver commanded.

The bus careened off the highway. The deep ravine was a few yards away, at least six feet across and hundreds of yards long. We skidded downward, the driver attacking the ditch head-on. Dirt wedged against the windows.

A flock of birds had been sheltered in the ravine. As we barged in, the birds lifted in fright. I watched them rise — and then I saw it. Unlike anything I'd ever seen before. It was startling, to see one firsthand, after having seen so many photographs. Like the finger of a dark and evil god. A swirling column, dropping from the sky. The startled birds flew into it. Right in front of my eyes, I saw their feathers peel off, I heard their deathly shrieks. Lifeless, naked carcasses flew everywhere. One shot right toward the front window.

"Down!" Stieg cried again. The driver cowered under his seat. I crouched down and heard the impact of birds and debris on the bus's metal frame.

Stieg remained standing.

The wind was loud now, like hundreds of lawn mowers flying through the air. The noise of chaos. I grabbed at Stieg's leg and tried to pull him to the floor. He wouldn't budge.

"Stieg!" I yelled above the din. I stood, in order to bring him back down. Both his hands were pressed against the windshield. I could not help but follow his gaze. The twister was no more than thirty yards away from us. I could feel it pushing — I could feel the Doppler waves pushing through the air. The cloud took on the color of the earth. Dirt rained in hard pellets.

Stieg's expression was one of utter amazement.

"Get down!" I ordered. Stieg nodded.

Then the floor began to lurch below us. As if succumbing to a magician's powers, the bus — all three tons of it — began to levitate. A few of the other passengers were whimpering now. I tackled Stieg and pinned him to the floor.

"No — I have to see!" he protested. But I would not let go of him.

Windows began to shatter. Glass rained down on our backs. I could hear the pulling of metal, and could only pray that the ground would keep hold of us. I half rose to look at the other passengers and saw two objects flying toward me. *Knitting needles.* I slammed back to the floor, just as the needles crashed against the front window, puncturing it.

I closed my eyes, but it was impossible to shut out the flashes of lightning. I could still hear, too — the horrible clamor of a world torn apart.

Then the noise began to ebb. The bus began to settle. A more normal rain began to fall. Stieg was the first to stand. The bus driver was sobbing. As Stieg gazed at the devastation, I checked the other passengers to see that everyone was okay. Besides a few cuts from the broken glass, the biggest problem was shock. I tried to calm down as many people as possible.

The elderly knitter just stared at her hands, which had once been holding needles and yarn. "They just flew out," she said, shaking her head in disbelief. "I didn't even let go."

The man who had been sitting behind me had swallowed his gum and a good part of his composure. As soon as the tornado subsided, he ran to the bathroom.

Other passengers were crying. We all were astonished.

We were alive.

The sky began to brighten. It was all over, all gone. I made Stieg stand still while I checked him for any cuts or other injuries. He was fine. He could not stop staring at the spot where the tornado had been.

"It was beautiful, wasn't it?" he asked.

I touched him on the shoulder and spoke low, so no one else could hear.

"Is this it? Was that why we're here?" I inquired.

"No, that wasn't the one," Stieg answered, shaking his head. "That was just something that got in our way."

All my relief receded. From the look on Stieg's face, I could tell:

Next time, we might not be so lucky.

Next time, it was going to be worse.

And next time was going to be very soon.

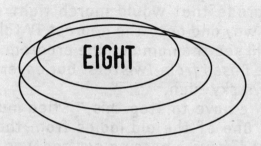

EIGHT

The bus was stuck in the ravine. The driver didn't even try to get it out. Instead, he focused on us — particularly Stieg. As I evacuated the other passengers, I kept turning around to see the driver staring in disbelief.

"How did you . . . How could you . . . You did, didn't you?" he sputtered.

"No, we didn't," I answered. "Just luck, that's all."

Stieg nodded in agreement and tried not to meet the driver's eyes. But wherever we turned, we only found other passengers looking at us.

We were in trouble. Not the kind of trouble that comes from doing too much bad. We were faced with the trouble that comes from doing too much good. Because as our fellow travelers got over the shock of the twister, their attentions turned to us. They tossed around words like "miracle" and "saviors." They looked like they'd form a parade at any moment. A parade in our honor, a parade that would march right down the highway and onto the nearest TV talk show. I could see the name of the program: *Kids Who Save Buses from Twisters.* Our cover would be blown sky-high.

"We have to stop this," Stieg mumbled to me. One of the old ladies from the bus had waved down a passing car and was now calling for help on a cellphone.

"We need to think of a lie," I said. And that's all it took. Stieg sprang up and asked for everyone's attention. The eleven passengers gathered at the side of the road, curious. I knew I'd have to play along. No matter what.

"You're heroes," one woman proclaimed.

Stieg shook his head.

"Look," he began, "I know this is going to sound unusual, but I have to say it. I have to trust you — my brother and I have to trust you. Because I know this is going to sound strange. Very strange. But you have to hear me out, and you have to help us."

"We're in your debt," the driver said gruffly.

"No, you're not. I guessed. I was lucky. But here's the thing: I know that all of you are going to want to talk about this. Heck, we've been through an amazing thing. But there's one thing I need you to do. Don't mention my brother and me."

"Don't be ridiculous," the woman who'd been knitting said. "Credit should go where credit is due."

"Not in this case. It can't. Ordinarily, I'd be willing to argue with you about it. But not now. You see . . . there's no way around telling you this . . . you see, my brother and I — our whole family, really — are in the witness protection program."

"No!" a few people instinctively cried out. They looked at me, and I nodded as gravely as I could.

"It's true," Stieg continued. "I'm not going to go into why. But our parents were federal witnesses — and there are more than a few people — *bad* people — who would love to track them down. And if our pictures — or even our names — get into the newspaper, or on TV — well, we're going to be in big trouble. Now, I know this is a lot to throw at you right now. But we've got to get our story straight. It's very simple. The tornado hit. Our driver swerved into the ravine and avoided it. THE END. It's not far from the truth. There was no advance warning. It just happened. Do you understand?"

All eleven people nodded. I studied their

faces carefully, and they all seemed sincere.

"Now, one of you has to tell the woman who's calling for help what our story is, okay?" Stieg wrapped up.

"Don't worry about Millie," one of the older men said. "She was asleep until we went into the ditch."

Stieg sighed. "Good. Look, we really appreciate this. My brother and I really appreciate it."

As he finished his sentence, the sound of sirens echoed down the road. Soon, an ambulance and a pair of police cars came speeding into view. We waited by the side of the road for them. I kept an eye out for Taggart. Maybe he had been close by for the tornado report. Maybe he knew we were here. I looked for somewhere to hide. But we were in the middle of nowhere. And it wasn't likely that the other passengers would let Stieg and me disappear. Not yet.

Stieg moved next to me. There was nothing more to do. We hung back and waited for any sign of the feds. We would run if we had to. We looked earnestly at each of the other passengers. Some of them nodded to us. Others were busy trying to pull their bags from the bus. As soon as the first police car arrived, an officer asked, "What happened here?" The driver stepped up and offered his version of events — *our* version of events.

Everyone agreed with him.

Soon, two more sets of EMTs had arrived. Everyone was checked for cuts and bruises. A few people were shaken up, but for the most part we were all okay.

Taggart was nowhere to be found.

We rode in ambulances to the nearest town. Word of our accident had obviously preceded us. When we arrived at the local hospital, there were no fewer than five camera crews waiting for us. (Which is, I imagine, a lot of camera crews for a small Kansas town.)

Taggart wasn't there . . . yet.

All chaos broke out — which was lucky for us. The reporters gravitated toward the bus driver (who had rolled down his sleeve, so his BUTCH tattoo wouldn't show). Then, looking straight at Stieg and me, one of the older passengers said very loudly, "OH MY LORD, I FEEL FAINT!" and began to stagger. This was all the diversion we needed. Grabbing hold of our bags, Stieg and I ducked our way to the nearest exit, leaving the commotion well behind us.

"Witness protection program," I groaned to Stieg as we faded from the microphones' earshot.

Stieg just smiled.

I couldn't believe he'd pulled it off.

"You're such a good liar," I said. Which

was both a good and a bad thing. On the one hand, it made it easier for us to get out of sticky situations. On the other hand, I always had to wonder whether Stieg would ever lie to *me*. And if he did, would I be able to notice?

"Excuse me! Excuse me!" someone yelled from behind us.

"Don't turn around," I whispered. A reporter on our trail — just what we needed.

"Please!" the voice, now more familiar, yelled. "I'm from the bus!"

I turned around, and found the woman with the knitting needles, nearly out of breath from running to catch us.

"Look," she began, breathing deeply. She appeared to be around Grandfather's age. "I don't believe your story. But don't worry. I just need to know one thing: Have you called your parents?"

She was looking at Stieg as she said this. And at that moment, I felt it would all fall apart. Because the question threw Stieg for a loop — *Have you called your parents?* I could see on his face the look he got whenever a stranger asked about our parents — the moment's hesitation of not knowing what to say, not knowing whether to go for the polite lie (*"Oh, they're fine"*) or the brutal truth (*"My parents are dead"*). It had amazed me when Stieg had said our parents were in the witness protection program — it had amazed me to hear him speaking of our parents out loud. But that had been in the midst of a lie. Now, this was in the midst of the truth. *Have you called your parents?* An understandable question. An impossible question.

"We're in touch," Stieg answered, looking sideways, looking anywhere but here.

"I see," the woman replied. But she didn't see at all. How could she?

"We're okay," I added, trying to reassure her.

The woman stared at us for a moment. Then she reached into her purse and handed us a business card: *SEW LONG, FARE WELL . . . Mrs. Harriet Goldsmith, Proprietor.*

"My store isn't far from here," Mrs. Goldsmith said. "If you need anything, please call me. I still don't know what you boys did back there. I'm not even going to try to explain it. Just please be careful, okay?"

Stieg and I nodded.

"All right, then," Mrs. Goldsmith nodded back. "I'd better go back. And you'd better hurry — you're going to be missed. But please, *please* call your parents."

"We will," I said, and it sounded strange, so strange. Stieg remained silent. After Mrs. Goldsmith had started to walk back to the hospital, Stieg and I ran in the opposite direction, to the nearest bus depot. We hopped on the next available bus and got off a few towns later. A room at the local Holiday Inn wasn't hard to come by. (Money talks.)

We were exhausted, but we could not rest.

We unfolded Stieg's cryptic sheet of paper, and began to explore.

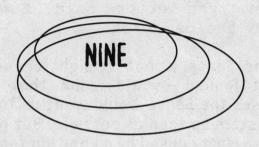

NINE

In the Chronicles, my great-great-grand-father had written:

The sense is not always CLEAR. It works with MYSTERY. The truth is always there. It must be FOUND. I don't know why this is. It just is.

Or, as my father wrote decades later:

I was seized. My hand moved — I grabbed a pen, and all I could draw was wave after wave. Endless waves. I didn't know what this meant. And then Laura came in and turned the waves upside down. Suddenly, they spelled "tomorrow." I could see them rising. I knew there would be a flood. And before I could wonder where, I saw other letters floating in the waves. I strung them together. I rearranged them. "Clarkstown," the letters said. I was there when the dam broke.

The Sense is not straightforward. Which isn't logical — you'd think that whatever causes the Sense would want us to stop the disasters as soon as possible. But maybe the Sense isn't caused by a knowing force. Maybe it's just the way my brother is wired.

Stieg and I stared at the map. Searching for direction, I was drawn to the arrows.

I arranged the letters according to the direction of the arrows.

Stieg stared and stared.
Then I realized.
Rotation.
I turned the letters in the direction of the arrows.
If there were two arrows, I turned the letters twice.

KENMORE.

I booted up my computer and checked an atlas.

Kenmore was almost two hundred miles away.

We were at the wrong end of Kansas.

"How much time do we have?" I asked Stieg.

He shook his head. "I don't know. Not today. But maybe tomorrow."

We had to move quickly.

I glanced at the rest of the map.

"Does any of this make sense to you?" I asked.

The woman without eyes. The number sequence. The spiral lines intersecting.

Stieg stretched out on the bed and closed his eyes.

"Don't go to sleep," I said. Stieg didn't move.

"Stieg?" I asked, more quietly. After a few moments, he sat back up.

"Nothing," he said. "I was trying to get it back. But I can't, okay? I'm trying, but I can't."

Stieg looked more and more frustrated with every sentence.

"It's okay," I murmured. Stieg turned away. It wasn't okay with him.

We gathered up our stuff. I made a quick call to the Hansens in Providence and asked them to call Grandfather and tell him we were okay. They would use safe channels.

Stieg and I were ready to leave. We had only been in the hotel room for half an hour.

"I must keep moving," my grandfather Edward wrote in 1940, on his way to an avalanche. "I must not stop. The Sense is telling me to move but all of my other senses are telling me to sleep. I keep driving and driving and I only stop when I have to. I am at a roadside diner now, here for my two bites. I don't dare to fall asleep. When I'm on the road and start to fall asleep, I hear the voices of the people going under. That wakes me up and I keep moving."

Like my grandfather, we could not stop moving.

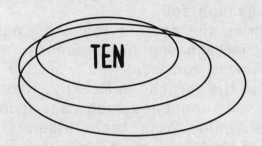

TEN

There weren't any buses to Kenmore. The lady at the bus station didn't even know where Kenmore was. Nor did she have any inclination to look it up.

Stieg and I moved to the taxi listings in the yellow pages. There were three taxis in the whole town. Two of the drivers laughed at us. (They seemed to know where Kenmore was.) The third sounded very skeptical. I ran to the nearest cash machine and used the ATM card my mother had left us. I knew I was taking a risk — Agent Taggart could have put a trace on our account. But since my parents had kept the account a secret, I hoped Taggart wouldn't be able to track it down. I withdrew as much money as I could from the cash machine. Then I called again and made my best offer. Sud-

denly the driver wasn't so skeptical anymore.

Soon enough, Stieg and I were on our way
to Kenmore. If we were lucky, we would arrive by nightfall.

During the drive, I told Stieg again about
the fierce power of tornadoes. What we'd
seen was far from the worst. I told him
about the tornado in Moberly, Missouri, that
had sent unopened soda cans flying eighty-
seven miles from their origin. I told him
about blades of grass that became bullets,
and glass shards that fragmented upon the
wind. Whole towns have been destroyed by
tornadoes. Libraries have flown. The strong-
est steel beams have been snapped like pret-
zel sticks. In 1931, a tornado threw a train
eighty feet off its track. The train weighed
eighty-three tons.

At best, the U.S. Weather Service can issue
a tornado warning eleven minutes in advance
of the drop. That's compared to days in
advance for hurricanes, or an average of
twenty-two minutes for a flash flood. Sometimes there's no warning at all. In early
1997, a tornado hit Alabama and a warning
wasn't issued until eleven minutes *after* the
twister had landed.

I stared out the window at the Kansas
landscape. I explained to Stieg that this was
the heart of Tornado Alley, the stretch of

land from South Dakota to northern Texas in which more than half of all U.S. tornadoes touch down. We were also in the heart of the tornado season, from April to June.

Stieg nodded after I finished explaining. I tried to watch his reaction closely. He asked me to stop staring at him. Then I looked in the rearview mirror at the taxi driver. My talk of tornadoes had spooked him out. He was driving much more carefully than he had been driving before.

"You sure are too young to be chasing them tornadoes," the driver said. "I see them folks all the time, with their fancy vans and their outfits. Clouds come in and they just roll all over town. Not fair, if you ask me. Drink all the coffee, throw all the cups around. Did you hear about the tornado that hit this morning? Nearly lifted up a bus, I tell you. Amazing stuff."

I nodded. Now it was Stieg's turn to stare out the window. The taxi driver wondered aloud how strong the tornado had been. This is something I had wondered myself. All tornadoes are rated on the Fujita scale, which takes into account, along with several other factors, the damage the tornado has caused. An F0 tornado is the weakest kind, with wind speed between forty and seventy-two miles per hour, a path length of under a mile, and a path width betwen six and seventeen yards. I guessed that the tornado we'd faced in the bus was an F2 tornado, with winds between 113 and 157 miles per hour, an average path length of six miles, and an average path width of thirty-six yards.

"It was an F-two," Stieg agreed, even though I hadn't asked him out loud. He knew this without any gauges or instruments.

My father had also had a sense for measurements. He could guess the accumulation of a snowstorm from the sound of the snow touching ground. I can remember him walking into my room when I had woken up before daylight — I can remember him telling me to go back to sleep because there was sure to be a snow day. Hours later, the phone would ring, informing us that school had been canceled.

I opened up a volume of the Chronicles, but found I couldn't read while the car was moving. So instead of looking to the past, I focused on the future. What would we do when we arrived in Kenmore? We couldn't just show up and say, "Hey, there's a tornado coming!" We'd be booted into the nearest loony bin. There had to be a better way. I just didn't know what it was. It wasn't something my father — or anyone else — had left guidelines about. We were given clues and examples, not step-by-step instructions.

Exits flashed by at twenty-mile intervals. Stieg slept. I tried to fight it. But soon enough, I was sleeping, too. Kansas disappeared. I saw spirals. I heard whispers, but couldn't understand what they were saying. Then I heard a voice, more clear, announce, "We're almost there."

"Did you hear me?" the taxi driver asked. I woke up. Stieg rubbed his eyes beside me. "We're almost there — Kenmore, Kansas. I won't ask why you're here. But I can't stay, you understand? You're on your own. I gotta get back."

I nodded and looked out the window. Nothing. Acres and acres of nothing. This was Kenmore?

There was a small sign:

KENMORE,
POPULATION 900.
WELCOME TO ALL!

Yes, this was Kenmore.

"I assume you want to be dropped downtown?" the driver asked.

"Sure," I answered, with more confidence than the word deserved.

"Where are we?" Stieg mumbled.

The "downtown" area was two blocks long. A service station. A market. A police station. A post office. A dress shop.

69

"Any particular address?" the cabbie asked.

I told him to drop us off at the post office. After I'd paid, the taxi zoomed back off into the horizon. The sun was just about to set.

"So now what do we do?" Stieg asked, peering into the opening of a mailbox.

"We go to the police," I said. I was re-membering something my father had written:

The police aren't always as cyni-cal as you think they'll be. Some-times they are, but sometimes they aren't. You can tell within a minute what their reaction will be. Usually they'll promise to keep an eye out on the weather, which is at the very least a help. Sometimes they'll send you away without another word. But generally it's a risk worth taking.

My father was thirty-one when he wrote this. I wondered if he would have been so sure of the police if he had been fourteen.

But I didn't have any other ideas.

"To the police station, then!" Stieg pro-claimed too jokingly, too loudly. I wasn't thrilled about his attitude. But at least he was awake.

The police station was no larger than a

convenience store. We stepped inside and walked toward what was obviously the front desk. A uniformed officer was arguing with a middle-aged woman about a parking ticket. He saw us approaching, halted the woman's complaint for a second, and asked us if we could take a seat. He would be with us in a minute.

"No problem, Officer," Stieg said. He and I walked to the only two chairs in the waiting area. The chairs were positioned between two open office doorways.

Stieg and I sat back. Judging by the look on the complainant's face, the officer was going to be busy for a little longer than a minute.

I looked at the Wanted posters. I was relieved to find that we weren't up there, newly faxed from federal headquarters.

My attention drifted. I didn't mean to eavesdrop. But the voices coming from the office to my right were hard to ignore.

"I'm telling you," a young female voice argued insistently, "a tornado is coming. Tomorrow. And if you don't do something, people could die."

"Now, Rachel," a second voice — older, male, equally insistent — said, "I understand your concern. But you realize I have no basis for any sort of action."

"I'm *giving you* a basis," Rachel (whoever

71

she was) yelled. "Don't you *see*? Are you *blind*?"

The male voice — a police voice — became curt. "*Don't* use that tone with me, young lady. I have indulged your father and mother heaven-knows-how-many times. But you're pushing it. I can't very well shut down the entire town because you have a *sense* that something *might* happen."

Rachel would not relent. "You could issue a warning," she insisted. "It can't hurt. I hope I'm wrong. But what if I'm right? It's better to be cautious — "

"You know very well that if I issue an alarm, this town will shut down," Police Voice interrupted. "Businesses will shut down. Schools will shut down. It will be chaos. And when the skies remain sunny, and there isn't a tornado in sight, it will be my head that's served on a platter." Police Voice calmed down once again. "Look," he said, "I'll keep a lookout. If the conditions begin to form, we will be notified immediately, and the proper measures will be activated. I will go to the tower myself and flip the switch with my very own hands. I can't do anything other than that. Now you should head on back to your brother. I fear, quite frankly, that he's putting all of these ideas in your head."

"It's not him that's putting the ideas in

my head," Rachel insisted. "It's something else. You have to listen to me."

"No, Rachel. I don't *have to* do anything until the first dangerous sign appears. End of discussion. Now please — head back home. Don't worry. If you have any other — "

Police Voice never had a chance to finish his sentence. Or if he finished his sentence, he did it to an empty room. The girl had already left. I caught a brief glimpse of her as she stormed out of the office. She looked about my age, with short brown hair and glasses. She didn't pause for any good-byes. Her departure was so forceful that even the woman at the counter stopped complaining and took notice.

I turned to Stieg, to see if he'd heard what the girl had said.

He was already out of his seat, following her out the door.

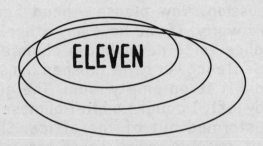

ELEVEN

"Wait!" Stieg and I yelled at the same time. I was calling to Stieg. Stieg was calling to the girl.

Neither Stieg nor the girl waited. The girl actually sped up. Stieg increased his pace to catch up with her. I was a not-so-distant third.

Finally, after Stieg had called out again, the girl stopped. She did not look happy.

"What?" she demanded. I thought Stieg would transform himself into Boy Charming in order to talk to her. (I had seen him do this thousands of times before.) But instead, he surprised me and stuck to the facts.

"We heard what you said in there," he explained earnestly. "We were going to say the same thing."

The girl's hair had fallen in front of her glasses. She blew it upward.

"Look," she said, "I don't know who you are. And I don't know what you're up to. But don't mess with me, okay? I have enough to deal with. I don't need to be teased."

She started to leave, but Stieg jumped in front of her.

"We're serious," he said. "There's going to be a tornado here tomorrow. We know."

The girl still looked skeptical. But at least she wasn't walking away.

"What are you talking about?" she asked.

"We know the tornado is coming," Stieg repeated. "We're from the East. But we came here because we know a tornado is going to hit tomorrow, and we want to help."

"How can you tell?"

Stieg shrugged. "I have a sense. It just came to me. It's something that happens."

"In your family?" the girl asked, her expression unsure of itself.

Stieg nodded.

"The Message?" the girl murmured.

"The Sense," Stieg answered.

I had to interrupt.

"What do you mean by 'the Message'?" I asked.

My tone must have been off. The girl was defensive again.

"Who are you?" she inquired.

"I'm Stieg," my brother answered. "This is Adam."

"I'm Rachel. Rachel Ede."

The last name felt like a jolt of lightning. Ede.

A family name that had often found its way into the Chronicles — and rarely in a positive light.

"An Ede was already here." "Norma Ede nearly had me killed." "The EDES are up to NO GOOD. I do not know why they always APPEAR, but they are RARELY any help."

Words that spanned generations. From what I had been able to piece together, the Edes were a family with a matrilineal trace of the Sense — meaning it was passed down from mother to daughter. The whole family — sons and husbands included — took the Ede name. One would think that my ancestors would have liked having another family able to help them fight disasters. But from what I could tell, the Edes were always after their own good.

My parents had never come into contact with an Ede.

But here I was.

Stieg must have sensed the change in my mood.

"What is it?" he asked. I ignored him and focused on Rachel.

"You're an Ede," I said.

It wasn't a question, but Rachel nodded anyway.

"Was your mother an Ede?" I asked.

Rachel nodded again.

"Was your father an Ede?"

This time, a shake of the head. No.

Just as I'd thought.

We were face-to-face with a member of the Ede family. One who had the Sense. Or the Message. Or whatever you want to call it.

"So do you know exactly when it's going to hit?" Stieg asked.

"No," Rachel admitted. She seemed more comfortable facing Stieg. I'd have to be careful about that.

"I only know it's tomorrow," Stieg offered.

"This is so strange," Rachel sighed. For some reason, I looked at her hands. Her fingernails were bitten to the quick. On her left hand, she wore a yellow Swatch with the word CAUTION written across it.

I wondered if we could trust her. I wondered what my parents would have done.

"So where are you from?" Stieg asked. "We've come from Connecticut. Did you have to come a long way?"

At this, Rachel actually cracked a smile. "I had to walk ten whole minutes to get here," she said. She paused to think for a second, then looked straight into Stieg's eyes. Her gaze hovered there. He didn't turn, and at the same time he wasn't afraid to blink. This seemed to satisfy her.

"Let's go," she said as she began to walk away. Stieg and I followed.

What else could we do?

"So what do you think?" Stieg asked as we walked toward the Ede house. "Is she cool?"

"I'm not sure," I said, outlining briefly the history of the Ede family, and how it intersected with our own family's circumstances.

Rachel Ede was walking too far ahead of us to hear. When she turned into a driveway, Stieg and I almost walked right by. She didn't wait for us before going inside. Instead, she left the door open.

"Look." Stieg pulled on my sleeve with one hand and pointed at the Edes' mailbox with the other. I stopped in my tracks. There was a sign from Stieg's map:

We were going in the right direction.
Or we were stepping into a trap.
There was no way to know.

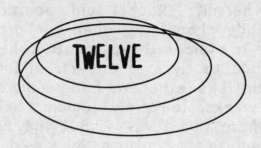

TWELVE

The Ede house seemed completely normal
from the outside. But the inside was totally
different. Rachel had disappeared. Stieg and
I entered the hallway and were faced with a
tornado chamber instead. It was the size of
a spiral staircase and took up the space in
the hallway where a spiral staircase would
have been. It was a glass tube, nearly three
feet in diameter and two stories high. Within, a diffusion of mist gathered in a slowly
churning funnel. It was strange and beautiful and entirely unsettling.

Stieg pressed his hand against the chamber, and I swear the tornado moved a few
inches closer to his touch. Through the mist
funnel, I saw a door open on the other end
of the tube. Rachel entered the room and
walked around to me and Stieg. She had

taken off her coat and looked a little calmer.

"My mother saw one at the Exploratorium in San Francisco and decided she had to have one herself," Rachel said, pointing to the tornado chamber. "When the artist came here to oversee the installation, he laughed. He had to fly in a crew from Los Angeles to put it together. We had people coming by for weeks. The crew couldn't believe how nowhere this town is, but they were paid enough to stay until the job was done."

"It's cool," Stieg commented.

"Yeah, I guess it is," Rachel agreed. "But it's entirely misleading. It's just designer steam."

"You can't bottle a tornado," I said.

"*Exactly,*" Rachel insisted. Then she shifted gears. "I suppose you should meet Zach. He's downstairs."

Stieg didn't want to budge from the tornado chamber, but I prodded him into following Rachel. We walked down a spiral staircase, painted black and lit by tiny lights planted unevenly throughout the wall. It was like walking across the ceiling of a planetarium.

"Let me talk, okay?" Rachel said before opening the door at the bottom of the stairway.

"No problem," I assured her.

As we walked into the basement, I was entirely amazed. I felt the way I feel when someone says exactly what I want to say, before I have a chance to say it. The Edes' basement was almost completely a replica of our Nerve Center. Satellite links. Two computers, one printing out reports from the National Severe Storms Forecast Center. A television showing the Weather Channel. A box of gauges. A barometer lying ready on the floor.

Amazing.

There was one difference from the Nerve Center: a lime-green couch sitting in the middle of everything. On it, a seventeen-year-old guy was sleeping with a baseball cap over his face.

"Zach," Rachel yelled.

Zach sat up quickly. His cap flew to the end of the sofa.

"HERE!" Zach shouted, although it was clear that he still didn't know where "here" was. Then he saw his sister and settled back down.

"I wasn't napping again, was I?" he asked Rachel.

"It was more like sleeping," she answered.

"Good." Zach reached out and pulled the cap back on his head. Instead of a team logo, the cap read, THINKING CAP (DO NOT REMOVE).

Zach began to stretch out his arms. He saw us midstretch and held his position a second before asking, "And to what do I owe this pleasure? Am I chaperoning a play date?"

"They say they know about the tornado," Rachel said. "They heard me talking to Chief Fontecchio." (Aka Police Voice.)

"And what did the good Chief have to say?" Zach yawned.

"He said a lot that amounted to nothing," Rachel reported.

"He didn't take you seriously?"

"He didn't even close the door while I was talking to him. I think our dear parents have exhausted his patience."

"Our parents? Has he seen them lately? If he does, I hope you told him to say hello for us."

Rachel sighed and turned the conversation back our way.

"He says he has the same premonitions I have," she said, pointing to Stieg. Then she turned to me. "And he, I think, is along for the ride."

"Not true," Stieg interjected. "He also pays my cab fare."

"Thanks," I said, with no effort made to control the edge in my voice. I hoped it cut him just enough to make him feel sorry.

"So hey — love and peace, you know?" Zach said, standing now. "Let's start acting

F-zero, okay? 'Cause yesterday we had an F-two 'cross state, and tomorrow we might have an F-six in our backyard, and I'm just not down with that, okay?" He walked over to one of the computers and hit a few keys. "Look," he reported, "the barometer is holding steady and the temperature is four degrees higher than it was two TV shows ago, so things are groovy for now. But they could go ballistic at a moment's notice. Comprende?"

"What he means," Rachel explained, "is that if the barometer is stable and the temperature is rising — "

" — there won't be a storm in the immediate future, because storms only form when the barometer drops and the temperature isn't rising," I interrupted. I didn't want her to think I was only "along for the ride."

"Okay," Rachel said, sitting down on the lime-green sofa. "I think it's time for a plan."

I wasn't entirely convinced that Stieg and I could trust the Edes. I wasn't going to tell them about the Chronicles, or about Stieg's map.

Stieg, however, was unpredictable. I had no idea what he would say.

"How do you know?" he asked Rachel. At first, I couldn't figure out what he meant. But Rachel knew immediately. It was time to put up or shut up.

"Words," she explained. "I hear and see words. Whenever I sleep. Sometimes even when I'm awake, daydreaming. Mostly it's garbled. But sometimes it's very, very clear. Like for this one, maybe because it's so close. A voice, saying 'tornado.' Loudly. And I keeping seeing the word — TORNADO — it's printed in front of whatever I'm looking at. TORNADO. Then a number. At first, I didn't know what the number meant. TORNADO TWELVE. TORNADO ELEVEN. Then I realized it was a countdown. The number decreased by one every time a day passed. This morning, it was down to TORNADO ONE."

"Tomorrow's ground zero, man," Zach enthused. Then he typed some further commands into the computer. E-mail.

"He's telling his friends," Rachel sighed. "He's a storm-chaser. Strictly amateur."

"But I'm a good amateur," Zach shot back.

"Yeah," Rachel deadpanned, "he can photograph rain like no one else in this town."

Zach swatted her comment away with a wave of his hand. He continued to type.

"So how did *you* know?" she asked Stieg. Stieg answered in detail. Before I could stop him, he'd mentioned the map.

Rachel asked if she could see it. I hesitated.

"I'm not so sure that's a good idea," I explained. I wanted to sound firm, but it came out lame.

"Hand it over," Rachel demanded. Which made me want to share even less.

Zach stood up from his computer. "Look, man," he said, "we don't have time for this. We're at the crossroads. The juncture. Either you're in or you're out. And if you're out, then you're out. We can't play games. 'Cause if we do, big mama twister is going to blow into town and whip us out of shape."

"You don't understand," I said. "Our families have been rivals for generations. I can't simply start trusting you now, just because you let us into your house."

"What are you talking about, 'rivals for generations'? Is your family from Kenmore or something?" Zach asked.

At that moment I knew: The Edes didn't have any kind of family chronicle. They had no link to the past. They didn't know.

I tried to explain.

"But why does it matter?" Rachel said after I'd finished. "That's them. We're us. That's . . . that's . . . *inarguable*. So just let it stop right here. I'm sure — and your brother's sure — that a tornado is going to hit here in the next twenty-four hours. I know you're from far off, but I've lived here all my life, and if that tornado hits, it's going to be destroying *my* house and *my* school and it could very well kill *my* friends and *my* neighbors. So my major concern right now isn't telling you over and over again that you can trust us. You'll just have to take my word and get over it. Because my major concern is saving as much as possible from the twister's path. Now *help*. Okay?"

Zach and Rachel looked to me with an imploring impatience.

"Just give her the paper," Stieg said.

Three against one.

I handed over the paper.

And as I did, I hoped against hope that the Edes would take one look at it and would see things that Stieg and I hadn't been able to see. It would make total sense to them, and the town would be saved.

But that's not what happened.

Zach and Rachel looked confused. Stieg pointed out the letters and the arrows and told how they had led us to Kenmore. The Edes were more than a little surprised to see their mailbox logo on the page. But they quickly moved past it and focused on the things we hadn't recognized.

"Classic storm formation," Zach said, gesturing to the spiral across the paper. He couldn't make sense of the lines in the corner, though.

Minutes passed. We didn't get anywhere. Zach offered us some Dr Pepper and faxed the map (over my objections) to a few of his storm-chasing friends.

"All right." Rachel pushed her glasses up and sighed after the map had been retrieved from the fax machine. "We have to think. This isn't enough to convince the Chief. We have to come up with another way. There are less than four hours until tomorrow."

"In the police station, when you were talking to the Chief, someone mentioned a tower," Stieg offered.

"Yeah," Rachel replied, "the warning tower. The minute it goes off, the whole town knows to duck and run."

"We could try to set it off," Stieg said.

"But if you activate the tower early, everyone will think it's a false alarm," I pointed out. "They'll go back to whatever they were doing, and might even ignore the next alarm."

"Exactly what I was thinking," Rachel seconded. "Plus, the warning system is coded. Only Chief Fontecchio and the mayor have the code. So we need an alternate route. The way to do it might be through TV. I mean, call Channel Two and Channel Four and Channel Eight and tell them what's going on."

"They'll never believe us," Zach shrugged.

"Even if they don't believe us, they'll put us on. And if that prepares more than one person, it will be worth it."

"No it won't," I disagreed.

"What do you mean?" Rachel asked.

"You're thinking short-term," I said. "In the long run, you're giving everything away." I told Rachel and Zach briefly about Agent Taggart.

"The Feds?" Zach wowed. "No kidding. That's some serious baggage."

Rachel steered the conversation back to the present dilemma.

"But what if there *is* no long term?" she asked. "What if this is a one-shot deal?"

"I have more than twenty notebooks saying it isn't," I stated.

"We have to alert the media." Rachel remained steadfast. "It's the only way left."

Now it was my turn to sigh. I knew right then: Even though it might take up time we didn't really have, I had to tell Zach, Rachel, and Stieg about what happened to my grandfather's brother.

I had to tell them what happened to Winston Atwood. Also known as Weather Boy.

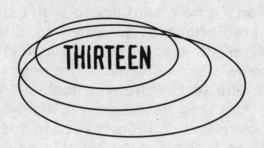

THIRTEEN

From the beginning, Winston Atwood's parents — my great-great-grandparents — knew he was going to be trouble.

"Jacob and Winston are both showing outstanding CAPABILITY in family matters," Christopher Atwood wrote in 1910, when both Jacob and Winston were ten years old. "Jacob has TALENT. He will excel. Winston is another matter altogether. I fear for him, as I fear for what he might do."

Winston and my great-grandfather Jacob were twins. They both had the Sense. Their parents recognized this from the very beginning.

When they were fifteen, Jacob and Winston were taken to see a forest fire. Jacob captured his reactions in the Chronicles. Winston did not record his response, which his father noted with disappointment.

Both Jacob and Winston fought in World War I. Both were lucky to survive. It was on the battlefield that Jacob's gift sharpened; his predictions of weather conditions contributed to his division's tactical success. Winston's Sense went in the opposite direction. The farther he was pushed from America, the less he perceived. He would never get over this abandonment. In the midst of war, he lost his most reliable powers. After he returned home, he would barely speak to his father and his brother. When he did, he never spoke of the Sense.

Strangely enough, Winston's Sense returned, informing him about a big 1919 drought, as well as a flood that killed twenty people in Arkansas. Sadly, Winston did not share his premonitions. By the time his Sense became clear to others, it was too late for anyone to be saved. Christopher Atwood berated his son repeatedly. ("How DARE HE deny his given ABILITY?" the elder Atwood wrote in the Chronicles.) At the age of twenty, Winston left home for good. The rest of the family doubted he would be able to make a living in the outside world. (He hadn't trained for any trade.) But Winston had already figured out what he'd do.

Winston traveled to Providence, Rhode Island, where he became a featured attraction in Dr. Fowler's Modern Fantasy Forum. At first, Dr. Fowler was skeptical about the Sense; he waited until Winston had correctly predicted the weather for a two-week span before making him a part of the Forum. In the 1920s, Providence was at the edge of the freak show and carnival circuit. Winston soon found himself traveling westward. He gained a new name — Weather Boy — and much notoriety. He went public with the Sense in a big way. Reporters waited at his every step. His advice was heeded by everyone from gardeners to governors.

Back home, Christopher Atwood read about his son's progress with much cynicism. "It is a disturbing notion to see Winston PARADE his GIFT for all to see," he wrote. "Soon they will not see CLEARLY, and NEITHER SHALL WINSTON. He is too EXPOSED. His actions expose US ALL."

Reporters trailed the other members of the Atwood family. Wherever they went, towns were evacuated — everyone thought their presence foretold a disaster. For that one short summer, Weather Boy enthralled the nation. But Winston began to have trouble keeping Weather Boy afloat. His Sense started to dim. Celebrity was worse than wartime. Winston made errors. He made enemies. And soon, his Sense was silenced.

Dr. Fowler begged Winston to revive his talent. Barring that, he asked Winston to fake it. But Winston didn't have even the faintest idea of how the weather worked; his father and brother had studied to gain that knowledge, while Winston had looked on with disdain. Weather Boy was soon finished. He was a freak without the gifts of a freak. Winston plunged into despair. He returned home, but it was too late.

Jacob Atwood, age twenty-two, saw his brother and wrote these words:

My brother is a destroyed man. He stares with blank eyes. He begs for me to tell him what I know. But I cannot. I cannot tell him of my feelings, for fear that I will become as empty as he. He does not know the weather anymore. He brings an umbrella in the sunshine. He does not notice the snow. He stays in the house and asks me what it is like outside. Even looking out the window, he does not know.

In the heart of the winter, Winston ran outdoors wearing only a swimsuit. He stayed outside for hours, until Jacob discovered him shivering by the side of a pond. Within an hour, Winston had contracted pneumonia. Within four days, he was dead.

Neither Jacob nor his father wrote about Winston's death. The Chronicles are not the place for such things. Like my parents' death, Winston's end remains on the missing pages. And yet its legacy can still be found in writing, days and years later.

Perhaps my great-great-grandfather had summed it up best. Two weeks after his son's death, Christopher Atwood scrawled four short sentences into the Atwood Family Chronicles:

The Sense KNOWS. It will not be ill-used. I guess we have learned. The Sense must remain a secret.

This is what I had to make clear to Stieg and Rachel and Zach.

The Sense must remain a secret.

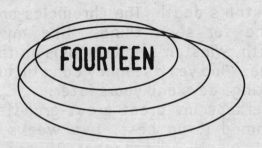

FOURTEEN

I paused for a moment after telling Rachel, Zach, and Stieg about Winston Atwood. I was especially attuned to Stieg's reaction. I had never told him the story. Many nights I'd started, but he hadn't seemed interested.

We all sat in silence for a moment. I couldn't read Stieg. Rachel's expression was a little easier — it was clear she had something to say; she was just trying to find the right words with which to say it.

Zach's reaction was the most obvious of all. "Whoa, man," he said, removing his cap and then putting it back on. "It's a miracle that Mom's sense didn't dry up long ago."

Rachel shot him a look that shut him up quick. But I held for a moment on his comment — did it mean his mother was like Winston — using the Sense for money and fame? I detected a note of anger in his voice. Clearly, he felt his mother's talent could be used for better things. Before I could ask a follow-up question, Rachel hijacked the conversation.

"So you're saying that nobody can know?" she stated.

I nodded.

"So how can we help?" she asked.

I told her what I thought: We had to keep watch. As soon as the weather began to turn, we had to raise the alarm. In the meantime, we could try to decipher Stieg's map. And we could try to prepare the town.

"What do you mean, *prepare the town?*"

"Well," I sputtered (since sometimes I say things without actually knowing what I mean), "we could slip tornado tips under people's doors, or in their mailboxes."

Rachel laughed.

"This is Tornado Alley, Adam," she said. "We've been hearing what to do in case of a tornado since before birth."

"Like opening windows?" Stieg asked.

"Wrong. Nope. You lose!" Zach crossed his arms into an X and made a sound like a game-show buzzer. "That's exactly what you *shouldn't* do. People used to think that buildings exploded because of excess pressure. But the truth is that the damage is caused by crazy high winds. So if you open the window, you're just letting the mess in."

"If the tornado hits," Rachel continued, "you head for the basement. If there isn't a basement, you go to the bathroom or any other central room of the house. The bathtub is especially safe, since the plumbing keeps you grounded. You have to stay away from outside windows, which can shatter, and outside walls, which can collapse."

"And everybody knows this?" I asked.

"I sure hope so," Zach sighed.

"You should also stay out of cars," Rachel stated, looking straight at Zach. "If you're in a car, you should get out and lie down, with your hands behind your head."

"Tornadoes are killer," Zach said, not quite looking at Rachel. "Last year, I was in Missouri, where this F-three landed. It was awesome. I mean, it was awful. But it was awesome, too, you know? Treated houses like firewood. This one lady — she was sleeping with her baby when she heard the tornado coming. So she just grabbed the kid and grabbed hold of the mattress and sure enough, the tornado ripped them right out of the bedroom and they landed *across the street*. They never left the mattress and luckily the winds didn't turn it over. So they had a cushioned fall. Across the street."

I remembered seeing footage of this twister on the news: telephone wires turned into clotheslines, the community center looking like a big haystack made out of wood. I wondered if it would have been any different if my parents had been alive. If maybe they would have known. They might have gotten there in time to evacuate the community center auditorium. Big rooms are the worst place to be in a tornado. They tend to collapse. Just like the community center did. Thirteen people were killed, in just under three seconds.

Now I wondered if there was any way for Stieg to have known ahead of time about that tornado. Or if Rachel had known. From their silence on the subject, I had to assume that neither could have predicted it — their Sense wasn't fully operational back then. But was it now?

An insistent beeping brought me back to the present. Zach went over to his computer and fumbled with the keys.

"What does that mean?" Stieg asked.

"Just an alarm," Zach answered. "It's now past midnight. Tomorrow is today."

"Tornado zero," Rachel whispered. It looked as if all of her energy had drained from her. Stieg also looked exhausted.

"Maybe we should take shifts," I offered. "Zach and I can stay up and watch the instruments. If there's any fluctuation in the barometer, we'll wake you up."

"It's all right," Rachel protested, stifling a yawn. "I can stay up."

"Look," I said, "we need you to be awake and alert. Right now, you probably wouldn't notice if the sky turned green."

I thought Rachel would put up more of a fight. But instead she said fine and made us promise we'd wake her if *anything* happened. She was going to sleep in her room for a couple of hours. Stieg would stay downstairs and rest on the couch.

It didn't take long for Stieg to fall asleep. Zach caught me watching Stieg in his REM state.

"Long day, huh?" Zach asked.

It had been the longest. The longest I could remember.

I turned to Zach and his computer.

"Any word from your friends?" I asked.

Zach shook his head.

"No dice," he sighed. "They can't make out your brother's map any more than I can. It's just totally whacked. The numbers on the side don't make any sense. And the woman without the eyes — well, that's just freaky. It can't mean that there won't be an eye to the storm, because there's *always* an eye to the storm. Although with tornadoes, you rarely see the eye. It moves too fast. And it will tear you apart before you get to the center."

"Have you always followed tornadoes?" I asked.

Zach shook his head. "Nope. My parents weren't too keen on the idea. But then I got a driver's license and there was very little they could do. It's not like they're ever around. They've got their own agenda, and we've got ours, I guess. I'm glad you guys are down with saving lives. My parents aren't like that. The best thing I can say about them is that they got me into tornadoes.

"I know it sounds geeky, but I just love the *science* of the thing. A tornado seems so simple — like water spinning down a drain. But it's so *complex*. We're learning so much about so many things, but tornadoes remain *unknown*. We have to track them down. It's like what those scientists — you know, Wurman, Straka, and Rasmussen — do with their radar in the center of a twister. The winds are blowing one hundred and sixty miles an hour, there's more than a hundred and thirty feet of pavement that's being stripped right off the ground and lifted into the air, cars are being hurled six hundred feet — and the scientists are *less than two miles away*, reading the tornado for, like, twelve minutes. That's *genius*, man. There's nothing in life like that."

"So you try to catch the tornado with a radar?" I asked.

"Not me," Zach sighed. "Not yet. But, yeah, the scientists use their Doppler. It's really cool. Because usually radars can't measure dry air. But there's so much rain and hail and other stuff flying around in the tornado that the airstreams can be read by the Doppler beams. Then the scientists can try to figure out what makes a tornado tick. They don't even pretend to be close to coming up with a way to *prevent* tornadoes. If anything, they'll be able to lengthen the warning time by another five to fifteen minutes."

Zach hit a few more keys and suddenly we were looking at the National Severe Storms Forecast Center's forecast radar. ("In through the back door," Zach muttered.) We zoomed into western Kansas, but couldn't find much to confirm what Stieg and Rachel knew. A storm system was approaching, but nothing that looked like more than rain. It *was* on a cold front — more conducive to tornadoes — but that alone wasn't enough to go on.

"This won't even rate a watch," Zach said in frustration. A tornado *watch* means the situation is right for tornado conditions to form. A tornado *warning* means that tornado conditions have already been detected. A watch would be enough to make people a little nervous. But it would take a warning to get everyone to safe shelter.

While Zach continued checking the radar and other sources, I slipped to my backpack and pulled out one of the Chronicles.

I read. Buildings destroyed. A woman dying in my great-grandfather's arms. My eyes were fighting to stay open. It was late. Very late. Very early morning.

Zach seemed perpetually untired. He kept pulling off his cap and putting it back on.

"I have an idea," he said aloud, to no one in particular. I don't think he realized Stieg and I were in the room anymore. He began furiously typing E-mail. It didn't seem right to read it over his shoulder. So I walked over to the barometer he had set up.

The pressure was starting to drop.

"Um . . . Zach," I said. He kept typing. Then he slid over in his chair to check the barometer.

"Nothing noteworthy yet," he concluded. "Keep your eye on it."

I tried. I stared. And, I guess, I started to fall asleep. I woke up three hours later. Zach was still typing. He smiled when he saw me looking at my watch.

"Don't worry," he assured me. "Everything's cool. The barometer is dropping very gradually. No cause for alarm. Plus, I think I found out something neat. Just a hunch that might have paid off."

I walked over to Zach. He gestured to the numbers on Stieg's map.

"Five numbers, all double-digit. Coordinates, I thought at first. But no. Then it occurred to me — maybe it was some sort of code. On a hunch, I got in touch with a chaser buddy of mine — his father's a sheriff in Oklahoma. And sure enough, this guy tells me that the code for the warning system in his town is five numbers, all double-digit."

"So you're saying . . ." I asked.

"I'm saying that your brother's Sense might just have given him the code for the warning tower here in town. Or maybe it's for another town. Then again, maybe it's not a code at all. I don't know. It's just a guess."

I woke Stieg up and asked him if any of this made sense to him. I thought he might *know*.

But all Stieg could muster was an "I'm not sure."

Rachel returned to the basement and immediately headed for the barometer. Turning to Zach, she didn't look too pleased.

"I thought you said you were going to wake me if something happened," she protested.

"Nothing's happened," Zach argued.

"Then what's this?" Rachel insisted, pointing at the barometer. "It's dropped since I left. That's something."

Zach flushed. "I guess it's been going down so gradually we didn't notice how far it had moved."

"And have you looked outside lately?" Rachel continued.

Zach shook his head. The basement didn't have any windows.

"Not a star in the sky," Rachel reported. "The clouds are here."

"Did you — ?" Stieg asked.

Rachel nodded. "Tornado zero," she said.

We all paused to look at each other. Then we walked outside to the patio.

The sky was approaching dawn. Sure enough, clouds had come in.

"Should we go to the tower?" I asked.

"Not yet," Stieg whispered.

Rachel nodded. "There are a few things we have to do first," she said. And without another word, she lifted a patio chair.

The rest of us followed.

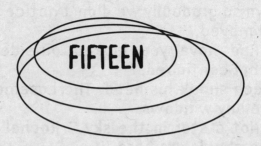

FIFTEEN

Soon enough, we were bringing in all of the patio furniture, flowerpots, and any other objects that weren't bolted to the ground. The twister's winds could turn any of these things into deadly missiles. The more that were packed inside, the better.

It was now definitely morning. But the sky had different ideas. It was still almost as dark as night. The clouds were thickening above. The barometer continued to dip. The wind was growing fiercer.

Stieg and I returned from checking the barometer to find Rachel on the kitchen phone.

"I'm serious . . ." she was saying. "You have to do it now . . . I don't care if you don't have confirmation. . . . No, I can't see your point. We're talking a matter of minutes. You have to give warning. . . . Fine. . . . Fine. . . . Oh, *shut up*."

She slammed down the phone.

"You just told the Chief of Police to shut up?" Stieg asked.

Rachel nodded.

"Cool."

Rachel brushed aside the compliment. "We have to get to the tower *now*. This thing could erupt any second."

Zach came running up out of the basement.

"I looked at the radar," he reported. "There's definitely a storm forming. The convection cell is forming. But I can't tell how." He turned to Stieg to explain. "In a normal thunderstorm, the convection cell is pretty much vertical. The air comes up the cell, but then rain forms and cools it down, halting the upward flow. But sometimes, the wind shear messes things up. A 'super cell' can form, which *might* generate a tornado."

"So from the radar's point of view, it's not a sure thing yet," I chimed in.

"Right-o," Zach nodded. "But we know better than the radar, don't we?" He smiled.

We were in the car in five minutes flat. Zach equipped it with a barometer and a temperature gauge. Rachel looked hesitant to leave the house. She kept touching things lightly as we headed for the door. At first, I didn't get it. Then I understood. She wasn't sure she'd ever see the house again. She wasn't sure it would survive the tornado. In the next hour, everything could be wiped out. Her whole house. Her whole history. It was amazing she could leave at all.

"C'mon!" Zach cried from the garage. We piled into his car.

"All right," he said as the garage door lifted, "now remember — I don't want any of us trying to be Evel Kneivel, okay?"

"Who's Evel Kneivel?" Stieg asked.

Zach smacked his head in mock agony. "You don't know who Evel Kneivel is? Man, that's just *wrong*."

"He's just saying not to take big risks," Rachel explained.

I wanted to point out to her that we were driving into tornado conditions in order to attempt to break into a government-owned warning site. Not exactly a low-risk situation. But I kept my mouth shut. We were going to take big risks. We'd have to avoid *unnecessary* ones.

It was a little after seven in the morning. The town was just waking up. Ours was the only car on the road. The air was filled with an eerie calm. Except for the wind. The wind was picking up, causing weather vanes to spin like records on a turntable. We passed the police station. A few squad cars were parked out front. Despite his refusal to listen to Rachel's pleas, I could imagine Chief Fontecchio watching the weather warily. He was waiting for official confirmation. But we didn't have time for that.

We were silent as we headed to the tower. I watched over Stieg, who seemed to withdraw further and further as the ride continued. He closed his eyes and his breathing grew erratic.

"What are you seeing?" I asked.

"A house," he said, not opening his eyes. "I see a house from above."

"Whose house?"

Stieg shook his head. "I don't know." He hit his leg. "I don't know."

"Stop," I said, before he could hit himself again.

"I hate 'I don't know,' " he whispered, opening his eyes.

"You can't know everything," Rachel said calmly. "Believe me. You want to know everything at once. You want everything to be so clear. But it never is."

"Here we go," Zach announced, screeching into the parking lot of the tower. It was a very strange creation — like a lighthouse in the middle of Kansas.

"Architectural fluke," Rachel explained. Then she ran around to the trunk and reappeared with a lock cutter.

"No time for pleasantries," she said, handing Zach the shears. We sprinted to the door of the tower and Zach cut open the lock. ("Sorry, Chief Fontecchio," he muttered.) As we walked up the twisted central stairway, Zach explained that there were two ways to activate the warning siren — manually, or through a phone code. Our job was simple — to activate the alarm and then disengage it from the phone system, so it couldn't be turned off immediately. The master alarm would set off sirens throughout the town. People would hear them and run for safety — we hoped.

The wind was beginning to howl. The walls shifted under its force. We reached the top of the tower and were faced with a dizzying view. The whole town spread below us, unaware. Above us, the clouds were growing darker. Their bottom surfaces had begun to churn.

"This is not good," Zach said, glancing out the window. "You guys should go back down. There's no reason whatsoever for you to be at the highest point in the county, just when a tornado's about to hit."

"I FOUND IT!" Rachel called from a corner of the room. And sure enough, she had — the controls for the siren. She opened up its casing and located the control keypad. I fed her the numbers from Stieg's map and prayed a

108

short prayer for them to work. Before she tapped the last number in, she told us to hold our ears. We did. She entered the last number. And then . . . nothing. Zach cursed. I removed my fingers from my ears. Just as I did . . . WAAAAAAHHHH. Deafening noise. Noise louder than a thousand rock concerts. A million TV test signals, all going off in my head. I covered my ears again.

Stieg was back at the window. I joined him. Rachel was right about the town — its residents were well-trained for disaster. Almost immediately, people began to run for their storm cellars. Rachel pulled the alarm's phone connection from the wall. We only had a few minutes before the police arrived. I looked toward the station downtown — the cars were still in place. Maybe the Chief was willing to let the siren go, as long as we took the blame. Or maybe he hadn't figured out yet that his phone connection had been severed.

Whatever the case, we had to leave. Because Zach was right: We were in the stupidest spot to face a tornado. Every wall here was an external wall. And we were seven stories above ground.

The winds were now blowing dust and debris around. From the window, I could see people having trouble closing their storm-cellar doors — there was too much wind resistance.

"Let's go!" Zach called. Rachel had already started down the stairs. Zach bolted after her. I followed. Then I looked behind me. No Stieg. I ran back up to the control room. He was still by the window. He had removed his hands from his ears. He was pointing. He was pointing at a house. *The* house. Zach and Rachel reappeared behind me.

"What is it?" Rachel asked. I was about to explain, but she wasn't talking to me. She was talking to my brother. The one with the Sense.

"That house," he yelled over the warning-alarm din. "That's the house I've seen."

"That's the Mitchell house," Zach said. "Mrs. Mitchell lives there. She's blind."

As soon as he said it, we all knew:

A blind woman. A woman with no eyes.

I pulled Stieg's map out of my pocket and thrust it at Zach.

He looked at the woman.

"Yeah," he said. "That's her."

It was her.

We were down the stairs in what seemed like a flash.

We had to get to the Mitchell house.

Before it was too late.

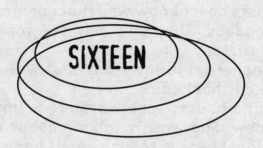

SIXTEEN

The thunderstorm began. The rain poured fiercely from the sky. Running the ten feet or so to the car, we were drenched to the skin. The wind howled relentlessly. As Zach peeled out, I could feel the car shifting under the force of the wind. Zach drove faster.

In the center of town, everything was quiet except for a pair of police cars making announcements, telling people to get to safe shelter. The emergency warning system was now in full operation. Chief Fontecchio could no longer deny the truth. Luckily, we had beaten him to it. There had been an earlier warning. Still, safety was far from assured.

"Do you know how to get to her house?" Stieg yelled. We were all yelling. The wind was too loud.

"It's by the high school," Zach answered.

The sky took on a greenish glow. And that's when I was certain. It was happening. I had read about the glow a thousand times — scientists don't know why it accompanies many tornadoes. They can only say for sure that it's there.

Rachel sat in the front seat with Zach. She looked shocked.

"The house," she whispered. Immediately I knew: She wasn't talking about our destination. She was talking about her own house. She was wondering whether it would survive.

Stieg leaned forward and touched her shoulder.

"It will be okay," he said. "Don't think about it."

It was yet another moment when I had to wonder: Where did my brother come from? How did he always know the right things to say?

I caught Zach's eyes looking in the rearview mirror. They were widening in surprise.

I turned to look behind us.

The southwest.

And there it was.

There was a churning bulge in the bottom of the storm clouds. The wall clouds.

Zach jammed down on the accelerator.

The wind flung dirt, dust, and grass against the windshield.

I watched out the back window.

Right over town, the tornado dropped.

And then, unbelievably, it was joined by another.

Two tornadoes. Thin. Gray. Unbelievable. They touched down to the ground and the dust and dirt and wood began to fly. No more than a half a mile away. Just outside the center of town.

"Just drive!" Rachel yelled, trying to prevent Zach from turning around to watch.

The twisters began their dance. There is no other way to describe it. One took the lead, then the other followed. A police car was lifted from the ground and shot into midair. The car's sirens were off; I prayed no one was inside.

The noise was incredible. Like a whole highway of cars crashing into each other.

Debris flew everywhere. Walls were reduced to planks.

Downtown was being shredded.

We were at a safe distance. But not for long.

One of the funnels pulled back into the clouds.

The other remained.

Gravel hammered against the side of the car.

The tornado plunged through power lines, causing sharp explosions of electricity.

Trees bent in the wind. All the branches seemed to blow to the same side.

We raced ahead.

We drove past the high school and swerved into the Mitchells' driveway.

"Get out of the car!" Zach yelled.

As we ran for the door, I turned around. The second tornado was fading. It was gone. But the rain still fell like bullets hitting the ground. And the wind was relentless.

It wasn't over yet. Even I could tell that.

Zach and Rachel pounded on the door.

An eight-year-old boy answered.

"Where's your mother?" Rachel yelled.

"She's upstairs," the kid answered. "Asleep."

Asleep?

"Look, man," Zach said firmly, "you have to let us in."

"Mom said I can't let strangers into the house."

Steig and I huddled on the porch. The wind and the rain were excruciating.

"This is an emergency," Rachel spoke up. Her voice was serious but kind. "The tornado is coming. You have to get into the basement. I'm Rachel Ede. This is my brother, Zach. And these are our friends Adam and Stieg. My mom, Mrs. Ede, was on the library committee with your mom a couple of years ago. Do you remember the woman with the red hair who came over to your house?"

The kid nodded.

"Good. That was my mom. So we're not strangers, okay? Now please let us see your mom."

The door opened further. Zach made his way inside.

"She's upstairs," the boy said again. "But you have to be quiet. She's asleep."

The wind picked up again. It sounded like a freight train hurtling off the tracks. Hurtling at us. "You two go upstairs and get Mrs. Mitchell," Rachel yelled above the noise. "Stieg and I will take — what's your name?"

"John," the boy answered.

"I'll take John to the basement," Rachel continued. "Okay?"

Zach and I didn't stop to answer. The two of us bolted upstairs. We found Mrs. Mitchell in no time flat. She was lying in her bed, oblivious to the world.

"MRS. MITCHELL!" Zach yelled. Nothing. I reached over to shake her. Just a little.

Finally, she stirred.

"What? Who?" she said. Instead of looking straight at us, as a seeing person would, she reached out her hands to touch us.

"Mrs. Mitchell, I'm Zach, Nancy Ede's son. There's a tornado about to fall. The alarm's been going for about ten minutes now. We have to get you downstairs."

"Where are the kids?" Mrs. Mitchell asked, now coming fully awake.

"Kids? John's downstairs. How many other kids are there?" Zach asked.

"Brady. We have to find Brady," Mrs. Mitchell screamed.

"We'll do that, Mrs. Mitchell," Zach answered. "You have to get downstairs now."

"*Oh my god . . . oh my god . . .*" Mrs. Mitchell felt around frantically for her cane.

There wasn't any time for explanations. Zach lifted Mrs. Mitchell into his arms and began to carry her downstairs.

"No!" Mrs. Mitchell cried. "Find Brady!"

"I'll find him!" I yelled.

"I'll be back up in a second," Zach told me. Then he was gone, down the stairs.

"BRADY!" I shouted, checking each room. I couldn't find him upstairs.

I ran down to the living room, near the front of the house. Zach and Stieg joined me there. Zach ran to the kitchen to look for Brady.

"Get downstairs!" I yelled to my brother.

"We have to find Brady!" he yelled back.

Something in the front window caught my eye. The storm was brewing again. The bottom surface of the cloud was churning. Yet another mesocyclone, ready to be riled by a wind shear.

I was paralyzed for a moment. Because I

could not escape the thought: *This was the last thing my parents ever saw.* A different time, a different place, but the same phenomena. This is what my parents saw before they died.

In the distance, trees were toppling over. I looked at the high school.

And that's when the next tornado dropped.

Stieg and I were knocked to the ground.

"Get downstairs!" I repeated.

"What's that?" Stieg yelled.

He pointed out the window at an object lifted from the high school. It was coming right at us.

"GET OUT OF THE WAY!" I screamed, grabbing my brother and throwing him onto the stairs. At that moment, the scoreboard from the high school football field crashed through the living room window, in an explosion of wind and glass.

Zach was running into the room as this happened. He recoiled just in time, shielding his face with his sleeve.

"ZACH!" I screamed. He uncovered his face. It was fine. But there was blood on his sleeve.

"HE MUST BE UPSTAIRS!" Zach yelled.

Immediately, I was back up the stairs, with Stieg on my heels.

"BRADY!" we both shouted. I plunged back

into the boys' bedroom. I nearly missed him. And then I saw a shock of blond hair poking out from under the bed. I bent over and swooped Brady up. He couldn't be older than six.

"It's going to be okay," I said. Truly a lie. Because at that moment I could hear the tornado outside. I could hear the glass breaking. I could hear the cars and trees and earth being pulled into the air.

There was no way we could make it back downstairs in time. The bathroom was our only hope. I ran as fast as I could into the next room and put Brady into the bathtub. I pulled some towels atop him and then covered him with my body, screaming assurances over the terrifying howls. Stieg fell beside me.

A horrible noise — even louder than before — drowned out my loudest words. The sound of a building being ripped apart. Even in a room without windows, the wind was upon us. Rain was upon us. The roof was being peeled from the house like the top of a sardine can. Rock and plaster and wood and rain fell on my back. Brady screamed. Stieg remained silent. I could only see the blurry outline of his face. He reached up and pulled the shower curtain down upon us. As the roof lifted away. As the tornado passed through us. We were in the heart of the wind. Near the eye of the tornado. It sounded and felt like a tractor was plowing directly over our heads. The sound was excruciating. The medicine cabinet shattered. The lid of the toilet was torn from the seat. I felt the wind pulling at me. I felt the shower curtain lift above my body. I grabbed the edge of the tub with all of my strength.

Stieg looked up. I looked up at Stieg.

And we both saw.

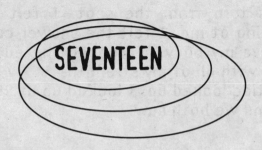

SEVENTEEN

It was amazing. As the tornado passed overhead, I watched. I had to. The shower curtain lifted in the air like a magic carpet. And then we were inside. It couldn't have lasted more than ten seconds.

We were in the eye.

We were caught in the funnel. The cloud walls churned, and yet were somehow smooth. Like if you touched them, they'd be smooth. Lightning was everywhere. Shooting from wall to wall, side to side. But through the lightning, you could look up. And it was all clear. All air. Up for more than half a mile. Like looking through a periscope into the sky. Getting a glimpse of peace before being thrown again into the walls. A brief pause before being torn apart.

I can't really explain what that moment was like. It was like everything was light for a moment.

Then I turned away, and the darkness returned.

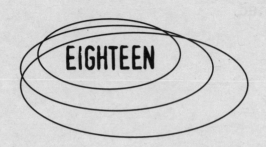

EIGHTEEN

It passed.

I stayed in the bathtub until the noise died down and Brady began to yell at me to get off of him.

When I raised my head again and took a look around, I could not believe my eyes. It was as if I'd woken up on a different planet. It looked a lot like the world I'd come from, only it was destroyed.

The rain continued to fall on us in the bathroom. The roof above us had been torn away.

I stood up, brushing off dust and pills and other remnants of what used to be the bathroom. Tiles had shattered around us.

I couldn't stop shaking.

A cry came from the floor below us — "BRADY!" — followed by more cries — Rachel and Zach calling our names. The rain died down. I was looking at sky. I heard footsteps trampling up the stairway. And suddenly everyone was in the doorway. Everyone was okay. Zach had some glass shards embedded in his arm. But otherwise, everyone was okay. Rachel was leading Mrs. Mitchell — nothing could stop her. She reached out for Brady and John and cried and cried. I started to sob, too. I don't know why. Relief, mostly. Relief and disbelief.

Zach grabbed me with his good arm and smiled.

"Well, Toto," he said, "I guess we're still in Kansas."

We left the bathroom and looked around. The top floor of the house was destroyed. Part of the roof had been pulled away. Brady's bed had been turned over and flattened. Drawers were opened. Clothes were everywhere. Even in the trees outside. All over the driveway.

I looked down. I expected to see the missing part of the roof right there. But it had flown into the neighbor's yard.

We left the house. Zach helped Mrs. Mitchell on the way back downstairs. We were afraid the house would collapse. And Rachel and Zach were anxious to leave. They wanted to see if their house was still standing.

Zach's car sat untouched. The driveway was littered with wood. Wood and debris that were formerly part of something, now unidentifiable. The scoreboard protruded from the living room window. The curtains were draped atop it.

We looked over to the high school, and saw only a shell of what the high school had been. A broken shell. Zach was speechless at first. Then he shook his head.

"One more hour and we would have all been there. That just freaks me," he said.

The weather had begun to clear. Only a light drizzle fell.

We made sure Mrs. Mitchell was going to be okay. We flagged down a neighbor, who came over to help.

"We have to get home," Rachel explained. Mrs. Mitchell didn't try to stop her. She was too busy holding John and Brady. Telling them it was all over. Telling them it would all be okay. Roofs didn't matter, as long as everyone was okay.

We got into the car and pulled out of the driveway. The emergency siren, we realized, had stopped. Now we heard other sirens. A multitude of sirens. Every emergency vehicle possible, swarming into the debris-strewn streets. Zach had wrapped his shirt around his arm. We insisted he go to a hospital, but he insisted on seeing his house first.

The signs weren't good. We passed the high school. The yard was filled with books and pieces of blackboard. A few people walked around dazed. Most, however, were carefully going through the rubble, making sure no one was inside.

We would have stopped to help. But Rachel and Zach needed to see their house.

Downtown was blocked off. The area was almost unrecognizable. A police car lay flipped over, like a beached whale. Rescue workers wearing orange armbands sifted through the wreckage.

We turned on the radio to hear the news. But all we could get were emergency warning signals.

Old news.

The top of the Edes' street was blocked by a fallen tree. Zach and Rachel abandoned the car and ran for their house. Stieg and I followed. We looked around, bewildered, at the remains of the homes.

At the beginning of the road, things weren't too bad. A porch dangled like a broken arm from the front of one house. Windows had blown out and the pavement was littered with glass and fragments of wood. Pets ran free as people hugged each other and stared at the ruins.

As we got to the middle part of the street, things became worse. Roofs had been torn away. Walls had collapsed. The lawns and pavement were now covered with more personal objects. Underwear. Silverware. A clock.

"I can't believe this," I said to Stieg. He didn't answer. He looked around and seemed to understand. This understanding didn't make him any happier.

Not much was left of the Edes' house. The front of the house had blown into the back of the house. That's what it looked like. Rachel and Zach stood next to each other. Zach's arm was around Rachel's shoulders. They weren't even crying. They were in shock. They stared, then turned away, then stared again.

"Everything," Zach kept saying. *"Everything."*

Stieg and I kept our distance. A rescue worker came up to us and asked us if everyone had gotten out of the house. She wanted to know if everyone was all right. After we nodded, she went and asked Rachel and Zach the same questions. She pulled Zach aside and took a look at his arm.

Rachel didn't move. She kept looking at the house, as if expecting it to somehow explain to her what had happened. Then she shook her head violently a few times and looked to the ground. An empty bureau drawer had fallen a couple of feet away from the house. Rachel bent to pick it up. Then she started to collect other things from the ground. She started to collect her house.

After a minute, Stieg and I bent over and began to help.

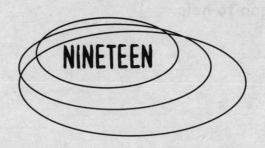

NINETEEN

No one had died.

When the warning signals stopped blaring from the radio, the first news reports came through: No one had died. Throughout the day, the same news was repeated. As more and more houses were searched, and more and more people were found, it appeared that no one had died. Thanks to an adherence to emergency procedures.

Thanks to an early warning.

There wasn't any electricity or running water left in Kenmore. There wouldn't be any for at least another day or two. And to make matters worse, the rain returned.

A quick census was taken in the town, to make sure everyone was accounted for. Stieg and I were listed as guests.

I kept expecting Zach and Rachel's parents to show up. But they didn't.

Neither Zach nor Rachel seemed too surprised about this.

"They're probably far from the news," Zach said.

"We've sent word out," Rachel added. "We can't deal with the insurance without them."

I wondered once more about the Edes — Rachel and Zach seemed to be trustworthy. But their parents were suspicious. Their parents fit the model of the Edes I'd read about in the Chronicles. I hoped I would never have to deal with them.

With their parents gone, Stieg and I helped Rachel and Zach in every way we could. In the spare free moments I had, I wrote in the Chronicles (which had survived the tornado in Zach's car). Much of the Edes' basement was still intact, as was some of the first floor. The second floor, though, was basically destroyed.

Every now and then, I'd catch Rachel staring or sobbing. I left her alone then. I didn't know what to say.

The whole town went around saying pretty much the same thing: They had been lucky, even though they had been unlucky. It was awful that so many buildings were destroyed, but at least everyone was okay. A few people had been injured, but after a few days, they were all out of the hospital. The nightmares would linger longer, but even those could be dealt with.

Through a member of the Network, Stieg and I managed to get word to Grandfather that we were okay. He sent word that we should come home soon. He missed us. Also, our school might get suspicious if we were gone too long. A weeklong vacation was about to begin. We'd have to return when it was over.

Agent Taggart had been by the house, but didn't seem to be hanging around anymore. Even if the house was under surveillance, there was a back entrance to the Maze that no one else knew about.

I wanted to go back to Grandfather. And at the same time, I didn't want to leave Rachel and Zach. Stieg didn't want to, either.

We sorted through the damage. We slept on cots that had been set up in the middle school. We ate food donated by strangers, and worked on the food lines in order to pay back our share.

While we worked and helped out, we heard all the town's tornado stories. One man had been standing on his porch trying to videotape the twister as it passed. He was thrown thirty feet into a neighbor's flowerbed. The video camera was never found.

Another man's car had been lifted through the roof of his garage . . . and landed in the middle of his living room.

Letters from the post office had been scattered more than twenty miles away.

The front window of the dress shop had been blown in. But somehow, the hats had stayed on the mannequins' heads.

A boy had found his baseball glove in his best friend's yard — three blocks away.

And so on.

These stories — and the mixed feelings of grief and luck — bonded the town together. Everyone told their stories. Everyone but us.

Rachel, Zach, Stieg, and I didn't even have to discuss it.

Our story would remain a secret.

Whenever Chief Fontecchio passed by, he wouldn't quite look Rachel in the eye. Even when he was talking to her, asking her if there was any way to track down her parents, he seemed afraid to make any sort of connection with her. He didn't know what to do.

Three days after the tornado, he approached the four of us while we were replacing the Edes' front door. Instead of looking at Rachel or Zach, he cast a glance over me and Stieg.

"Don't be going anywhere fast," he said, in a not-unfriendly tone. "There's someone flying in who wants to see you. Someone official."

I couldn't find the words to respond. I merely nodded. My blood turned ice-cold. Because I knew immediately who was coming.

Agent Taggart.

As soon as Chief Fontecchio had left, I told Rachel and Zach we had to go.

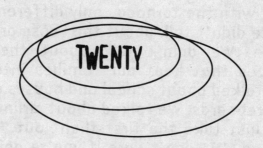

TWENTY

Zach drove us to the nearest airport (which wasn't nearly near enough). Rachel came along for the ride.

At first we were silent. There didn't seem to be words to express what we'd been through.

"What are you going to do now?" Stieg finally asked.

Rachel and Zach looked at each other. Then they burst out laughing.

"We have no idea," Zach said, shaking his head. "Absolutely no idea."

Rachel apologized for laughing. "It's either that or crying," she said. "And I'm sick of crying."

We talked some more about the future. About getting past Agent Taggart and going home. None of us knew what the future would be like, now that the Sense and the Message were making themselves heard so strongly in Stieg and Rachel. It was a scary and exciting feeling. Almost like what we felt with the tornado, only different.

We didn't talk about the Sense or the Message. We didn't talk about the strange forces that kept our families intertwined. We talked about school and houses and flying scoreboards. We talked about airline tickets.

"Just take the first flight out," Zach insisted. "I don't care if you're going in the wrong direction. Just get out of here. And then go home."

The tornado was still the top headline in the Kansas papers. It had been an F4, with winds over two hundred miles an hour. (Only one to two percent of all tornadoes ever get that fast.) Still, anyone looking at us in the airport probably wouldn't have known we'd been in the eye. Not the security guards who gave the four of us a passing glance. Not the ticket agent who had no idea when we'd spelled our last name as "Atwold" instead of "Atwood," in order to avoid any orders Taggart might have left on the airline's computers.

We booked a seat on the next flight out, to Chicago, leaving in fifteen minutes. Now that it was time to say good-bye, we really didn't know what to say.

I gave Zach the name of Marty Chester, a family friend in D.C. through whom we could exchange messages.

"Don't worry, we'll meet again," Zach said to Stieg and me. I didn't doubt it for a second.

Then it was time to go. Zach tipped his cap to us, and Rachel gave Stieg a kiss on the cheek.

Instead of saying good-bye, we told each other to be careful.

Stieg and I had to rush to get to the gate in time. We had only the bags we'd come with. That, and the biggest story of our lives.

As we settled into our seats, I studied Stieg. I'd never seen him so tired. I'd never seen him so down. I couldn't tell whether it was the good-byes, or the tornado wreckage, or the prospect of going home that upset him. I wanted to make sure he knew the significance of what had happened in the past few days.

"You know what you did, don't you?" I said. "No one was killed. No one was really injured."

Stieg looked glumly out the window.

"The Sense did it," he said. "Not me."

He drew down the window shade and closed his eyes. By the time the plane lifted off, he was asleep. I pulled out the Chronicles and tried to get down as complete an account as possible of what had happened. I couldn't explain all of it, but at least I could try to record events. Just as my father had done, and his father's father, and all the At-wood fathers beforehand.

Halfway through the flight, Stieg became restless beside me. Not violently. Not enough to wake up. But still, he shifted and dodged as if he'd been captured by a particularly bad nightmare. The shredding of buildings, the bursting of glass — these were the dreams that I had been having. For Stieg, they might have been worse.

When he began to mutter in his sleep, I expected him to say *help* or *twister* or *save me*.

But instead he said something different.

He said *earthquake*.

ABOUT THE AUTHOR

DAVID LEVITHAN is a graduate of the Wee Folk Day School, B'nai Jusheran Nursery School, Deerfield Elementary School, Millburn Junior High School, Millburn High School, Brown University, and the BSC Finishing School. He grew up in Short Hills, New Jersey, and believed for a long time that Hurricane David had been named after him. He currently lives in New Jersey and works by day as an editor in New York City.

ACKNOWLEDGMENTS

In the Eye of the Tornado is a mix of fact and fiction. For facts and tornado stories, I recommend the following works, which proved to be invaluable resources for this book:

Twister: The Science of Tornadoes and the Making of an Adventure Movie by Keay Davidson (Pocket, 1996)

Tornadoes! by Lorraine Jean Hopping, illustrated by Jody Wheeler (Scholastic, 1994)

Hurricanes and Twisters by Robert Irving (Scholastic, 1955)

Storms and Hurricanes by Kathy Gemmell (Usbourne, 1995)

"Unraveling the Mysteries of Twisters" by J. Madeleine Nash (*Time* magazine, May 20, 1996)

"Tornadoes" by Robert Davies-Jones (*Scientific American*, August 1995)

Numerous articles in *The New York Times*

On the fictional side of things, I would like to thank my family, Cary Retlin and *his* family, Shelly Veehoff, Bethany Buck, Janet Vultee, Helen Perelman, Karen Hudson, Craig Walker, and the BSC team for their help and encouragement.